MW00948699

Praise for Steve Alcorn's
A Matter of Justice

"Steve Alcorn is one of those writers who deserves success ... His books for young readers have a nice flair. I was favorably impressed ... she thinks and acts just like a girl ... it was a surprise, though the hints were there."
— *Piers Anthony, NY Times Best-Selling Author*

"Steve Alcorn cares and it shows as his teen girl detective, Dani Deucer, explores some of the same questions facing his own daughter, Dani. This is a good read for kids and adults alike."
— *Doran William Cannon, Screenwriter*

Steve Alcorn

Steve Alcorn is the CEO of Alcorn McBride Inc., a theme park engineering company. He also teaches writing through the online learning programs of more than 1500 colleges and universities, worldwide. He spent his childhood summers exploring the community of Three Rivers, California. He is the author of half a dozen books, including three novels.

Dani Alcorn is the inspiration for D. Deucer. When she was the age of the character in this novel, she visited Three Rivers and was mysteriously befriended by a stray dog while exploring "Mott's" bridge.

Also by Steve Alcorn

Everything In Its Path
(a novel about the St. Francis Dam Disaster)

Ring of Diamonds (writing as Sharon Stevens)

Travel Kid (a pictorial journal)

Building a Better Mouse:
The Story of the Electronic Imagineers Who Designed
Epcot

Theme Park Design:
Behind the Scenes with an Engineer

e-mail the author at:
steve@alcorn.com

A Matter of Justice

~~~~~~~~~~~~~~

Steve Alcorn

Theme Perks Inc.
Orlando, FL

Cover design by Dani Alcorn

Second Edition, July 2012

Theme Perks Press
www.themeperks.com

Printed in the United States of America

Acknowledgments

Thanks to my New York pen pal Steve Pisano for finding Dani's voice, to the members of YAWrite for the critiques, to my wife Linda for the encouragement, and to my parents for introducing me to the town of Three Rivers, California. And thanks to the real Dani for this awesome new cover design on the second edition.

Most of the places and incidental characters in this book are real. They are based upon the summers I spent in Three Rivers, California – particularly the summer of 1968. The murder and the mystery surrounding it are, of course, completely fictional. But I like to think that, faced with similar circumstances, I might have acted much as does the fictional Dani.

Steve Alcorn
Orlando, Florida
2003

Dedication

This book is dedicated to my daughter and steadfast bedtime collaborator, the real Dani.

Kaweah River
North Fork

Karp's Trailer

North

To Sequoia Nationa
Park (20 mi)

Kaweah River
Main Fork

Mott's Shack

Artists's
Colony

Kaweah
Post Office

Huffaker's
Country Candies

Trailer Isle

Swimming
Hole

Pasture

Three Rivers
Drive-In Restaurant

Clayton's
House   Barn

Rodeo
Grounds

**Three Rivers
California**

Library

Three Rivers Market

Sheriff's Office

Pat's Service Station

0   ½ Mile 1 Mile

To Visalia (30 mi)

Mockingbirds don't do one thing but make music for us to enjoy. They don't eat up people's gardens, don't nest in corncribs, they don't do one thing but sing their hearts out for us. That's why it's a sin to kill a mockingbird.

—*To Kill a Mockingbird* by Harper Lee

1. Mott

Mott Simon was the last person on this earth I wanted to see so soon after breakfast. But as I rounded the corner on my bike and headed into the library parking lot, there he was, half undressed in the heat, directly in front of the library door. There was simply no way to escape him.

At first, I put on my brake, and I seriously thought about just turning around and peddling the three miles back to the trailer. But the book was due, and I'd owe ten cents if I allowed my fear of Mott Simon to control me. So I let go of the brake with my foot and rattled down the last part of the hill.

I wasn't the only kid who felt that way about Mott. And I knew at least a few adults who felt the same way, too.

Mott Simon was weird.

Not just a little weird, but a lot weird.

Scary weird.

Okay, so I know I'm supposed to get to know a person first and not judge them by how they look or talk. My Mom and Dad have told me this a million times. And my 6th-grade teacher, Miss Read, practically tells us this every week, especially if she catches any of us making fun of Bobby Tollerude, the short kid with big ears and yellow teeth who always has his finger poked up his nose.

But as far as I know, they've never met Mott Simon.

For one thing, Mott Simon was as totally gross as a river rat. Ever been down to the river and have one of them pop out of the rocks as you're fishing for pollywogs, then scurry across your feet? Well, I have! I almost puked!

Mott's hands, and most of the rest of his exposed skin, were mud-brown with dirt. And the T-shirt he always wore, which must have been white once (and minus all those holes), looked as if it had been soaked in day-old coffee. His jeans, too, were dirty and torn. He looked like something a dog might have uncovered, digging on the side of the road.

But maybe the worst thing about Mott was he stunk of peat moss and grass and horse manure, like a farm animal. I don't know how he could even stand to smell himself, especially in the summer heat.

I know things are not the same in Three Rivers as they are back home in Los Angeles. But this was still California, wasn't it? People took baths here, didn't they? It certainly didn't seem like Mott Simon ever did.

Some people in Three Rivers called Mott a bum. Some people called him crazy. Some people called him things that, I must admit, I sometimes thought to myself in silence but would never have said out loud, even if I did ever talk to him, which I didn't. Nearly everybody in town seemed to have a strong opinion about Mott Simon – at least as strong as his smell.

Back home in L.A., people probably wouldn't have paid too much attention to a guy like Mott Simon. But Three Rivers was a mountain town, and not a very big one, and in Three Rivers Mott Simon might as well have been a Sasquatch – you know, Bigfoot. That's how much he stood out.

For starters, he lived up North Fork Road – not in a house, if you can believe it, but under a bridge near the river (like some kind of troll!). And no matter where

I encountered Mott in and around Three Rivers – over at the drive-in restaurant, up by the art studio, or here, in front of the town library – he always carried egg cartons cradled under one arm. Egg cartons filled with dirt.

He carried dirt around like it was his pet. Maybe he thought it was.

I was careful not to look at Mott as I stopped my bike. He was sitting in the middle of the flowerbed outside the library entrance. Around him was an array of flowers laid on their sides, their frail white roots showing. Mott looked like a big mangy dog, digging holes.

I gave him the usual wide berth, making sure to avoid any eye contact. As quickly as I could, I opened the front door, felt a blast of cold air-conditioning against my face and bare legs, then slipped inside. I was so glad Mott hadn't spoken to me.

Mrs. Peck, the librarian, was seated as usual at the large oak desk in front of the door. She was wrapping a crinkly cellophane sleeve over the cover of a thick book. A pair of pink-framed reading glasses rested halfway down her nose.

"Good morning, Dani," she said, taping a flap down on the book. "Back for more books, I see."

But I was distracted by what I saw out of the corner of my eye, and I wasn't really listening. Back through the front door, Mott Simon danced about wildly in the dirt, swatting his head with one hand while under the other arm he still firmly clutched his precious egg carton.

"What is he *doing*?" I said, rolling my eyes.

"Looks like another bumblebee is entertaining Mr. Simon," Mrs. Peck said. "It seems everywhere Mr. Simon goes, bees and flies follow."

Maybe it's because he smells like a cow, I thought.

"Mrs. Peck?" I said, "Do you think that guy is safe?"

Mrs. Peck stopped her work to look up at me, regarded me seriously, then shook her head in an ominous way.

Aha! I knew it! I knew Mott Simon was a weirdo and wasn't safe! I bet he was planning to kidnap me one of these days, and to drag me up to his disgusting little rat-infested shack under the bridge.

"I'm surprised at you, Dani." Mrs. Peck said. She stared at me hard, then her smile returned. "Mr. Simon is a very nice man. He's just...different, that's all."

You can say that again, I thought. But I didn't say anything to Mrs. Peck. It was all I could do to keep my smile from turning into laughter as I watched Mott run around in a circle, flapping his dirty arms, hitting himself in the head, still persecuted by the angry bumblebee who didn't think Mott should be rummaging around in the flowers any more than I did.

"You're just a visitor for the summer here, Dani. But most of us who've been living here a while know Mr. Simon very well, and we welcome him. And his talents."

His talents? I thought. His talents? For what? For dancing around in a flowerbed like a lunatic? For smelling like the inside of a barn? All the while Mrs. Peck was calling Mott "Mr. Simon," I was thinking, "Simple Simon met a pieman, going to the fair..."

"I'll grant you, Dani, Mr. Simon takes a little getting used to. But Mr. Simon can turn a garbage heap into a

Garden of Eden. The man knows something about flowers and trees that the rest of us will never know, even if we read all the gardening books in this library. Mr. Simon knows how to make things bloom."

"Yeah, well...he gives me the willies."

Mrs. Peck put aside the book she was working on. "Let's just change the subject," she said. "Are you returning that book?" She looked at the Nancy Drew book I held clasped in my hands like a hymnal.

"Yes," I said. I set the book on the desk.

"At this rate, young lady, you'll have read every book we have before summer is over."

"There's not a whole lot of action at our trailer, so I guess I'm getting a lot of reading done," I said. Back home I prided myself on my reading prowess, but Mrs. Peck's prediction was strangely depressing. Reading was my escape. What would I do if I actually *did* read every book in the library? Play with Stephanie? Yeah, right. That would be a laugh and a half. All my sister and her goofy friends liked to talk about were boys and clothes and music. I, on the other hand, had higher and more exciting aspirations.

"Got anything new, Mrs. Peck?"

"Since Monday? I'm afraid not, Dani. We're a library, not a newsstand. Though we may get some new books in a couple of weeks, I'm told."

The library was considerably smaller than the city library back home, but it still had a lot of interesting books. Half a dozen shelves stretched out in either direction from the librarian's desk in the center of the building. One side was labeled Non-Fiction and Reference. The other side included sections labeled Children, Young Adult, and General Fiction. Mr. Gruber, owner of the drive-in restaurant, sat in a sunlit corner reading the newspaper – or at least appearing to read the newspaper. I think he was sleeping.

I looked out through the glass of the front door again, but Mott's wild dance had ended. He'd resettled himself in the dirt and was quietly digging with a trowel. I guess the bumblebee had gone elsewhere.

I walked to the nearest bookcase and ran my finger along the shelf of mysteries. There weren't many, at least not as many as in L.A.

Read that. Read that. Read that, too. Shoot. I've read all of these.

"There's more to life than just mysteries, you know," Mrs. Peck called. Her orange flower print dress clashed monumentally with her curly red hair. She looked like a burning bush. "Louisa May Alcott wrote some great literature that I loved as a girl," continued Mrs. Peck.

I couldn't keep my eye off a particularly bright flower on the shoulder of Mrs. Peck's dress. The word "literature" made me bristle. It made me think of school, and I wanted to think only of vacation. Even though I had gotten all A's this past year (well, a B+ in phys ed), I didn't want to think about school on vacation. I'd be going into junior high in September, and Stephanie, who was a year ahead of me, frequently moaned about how much homework she had to do there.

"I'm on my vacation now," I protested. "The way I figure it, I can read what I like now and save that other stuff for school."

Mrs. Peck nodded. "I suppose I shouldn't be pestering you, dear."

Just then, a low roaring sound came from outside, getting louder and louder, making the library vibrate. It sounded as if a plane was going to crash into the building. But I knew there were no airports anywhere around. I wondered if it was an earthquake.

Even Mrs. Peck turned to look outside. Mott Simon stood, gazing out at the road, his hands clamped over his ears.

The roaring grew louder. And louder. Then we all watched (even a groggy Mr. Gruber) as a dozen or so large motorcycles drove slowly past. The riders were big guys with long dirty hair and red bandanas and black motorcycle jackets.

"Wow," I said, after they'd passed. "What was that all about?"

I had seen motorcycles like these back in the city, but they didn't seem as noisy there. Here, in quiet Three Rivers, it was like standing under a Saturn rocket. Mrs. Peck looked at me in a funny, shushing way. For some reason she didn't want to answer my question.

After the roaring ended, and my heart quieted, and Mr. Gruber went back to his paper and his nap, I moved on to the Hardy Boys section. I was disappointed to discover there were only a half-dozen titles.

"Do you have any more Hardy Boys books anywhere?" I asked.

I know it sounds silly, but I half-hoped Mrs. Peck might say, "Why, of course, Dani, we have several boxes of never-before-read volumes squirreled away in the back room – reserved only for our best readers, like you."

Instead, she opened the wooden three-by-five card file on her desk and flipped through the cards – her fingernails showing evidence that she chewed on them. One card for each checked-out book. There couldn't have been more than ten cards in the box.

"There's one title that hasn't been returned," she said.

My heart quickened.

"But it's been out so long I'm not sure it's ever coming back. Harold Dawson's parents split up at the end of the school year, and I think he's gone to San Diego with his mother. Probably with the book, too."

I craned to get a look at the title on the card, written in Mrs. Peck's small, curlicued handwriting.

"I've read it, anyway," I said. The ink on the card was a pretty, pale violet, like some of the flowers I had seen Mott Simon sitting among out front.

"Do you have 'The Big Sleep' by Raymond Chandler?" I asked.

Mrs. Peck's eyebrows rose above the frames of her glasses. "Even if I did, Dani, I wouldn't loan it to a young girl."

"I'm twelve," I said. "And anyway, I've seen the movie," which was true.

"I'm surprised your parents would allow it. I guess it's different, in the city."

"I guess," I said. But I didn't see why it was different. We weren't *that* far from the city. It's not like we were in Siberia.

Mrs. Peck rose from her desk and walked silently on thick-soled shoes to where I stood. "Here, dear, try this," she said, handing me a hardback book with its corners bumped up and a dark cup stain on the back cover.

"*To Kill a Mockingbird*," I read aloud. There was a picture of a tree on the front, and the author's name: Harper Lee. It sounded like they'd gotten the first and last names mixed up. I wanted to be tactful, but I also didn't want to read such a boring looking book. "No thanks," I said, trying to hand it back. "I don't think I'd like to read anything about killing birds. I love animals."

"It's not about killing birds," Mrs. Peck said. "It's about justice."

She must have seen I was unimpressed, because she added, "And it's also a detective story. Of sorts."

The "detective story" part of her description got my attention. But the "of sorts" part had me a little worried that we were talking about literature again.

"All right, I'll try it," I said. I didn't see much else on the shelves.

Then I had an idea.

"Would you have any books about how to become a detective?" I asked.

The question brought forth a genuine laugh from Mrs. Peck. It was such a pleasant and musical sound I found myself smiling along, rather than being offended, as I suppose I should have been.

"No," Mrs. Peck said, "No, I'm afraid we don't have anything like that." She folded her hands atop the book in front of her and gazed at me. "What is it with you and detectives, anyway?" she asked.

"When I'm older, I'm going to be a detective and work for the LAPD, or maybe for the FBI," I said.

"I see," she said.

I reached into the back pocket of my cut-off jeans, extracting a handful of items, and placed them on Mrs. Peck's desk next to her rubber stamp pad. There was a stick of spearmint gum, a wad of packing twine, and a nickel-colored washer I found on the sidewalk outside the Laundromat. There was also a white piece of cardboard the size of a business card, but cut somewhat unevenly. I handed it to Mrs. Peck, who held it at arm's length and peered at it.

"D. Deucer," she read aloud—perhaps a little *too* loudly because Mr. Gruber in the corner stirred again, and his newspaper rustled. "Private Investigator, #14 Trailer Isle, Three Rivers." She handed the card back. "Very impressive, Dani. Still, I suppose it takes more than a clever name to become a detective."

"That's exactly why I need a book about detecting," I said, "To learn the ropes. I'm good at puzzles. And I think I understand people pretty well. At least, that's what my folks say. I just need to learn some of the procedures, practice my skills, that sort of thing. You know?"

"I'm not sure how much detecting we need around here, dear. Three Rivers is a fairly quiet place."

"I don't mean just around here. I'll be going back to Los Angeles after the summer is over. There's lots of crime in L.A."

Even as I said that, I realized how awful it sounded. That was my home I was talking about.

"I would start with little things," I said, "You know, around school and at home. Like who trashed the teachers' bathroom, or who stole someone's lunch, or what happened to Dad's watch. That sort of stuff."

Mrs. Peck smiled. "It sounds like you wouldn't be very popular if you solved some of those crimes."

"Maybe not," I said. "But justice isn't about being popular; it's about doing what's right. You can't compromise justice."

Mrs. Peck's eyebrows rose up in thin red arcs over her eyeglasses.

"Compromise justice?" she said. "That's quite a sophisticated concept for a girl your age. Admirable, though. But I'm not sure justice is always as straightforward as you describe."

"What do you mean? Either something is right or it's wrong. It can't be both."

She picked up the copy of *To Kill a Mockingbird*, slipped the card from the pocket in the front, wrote my name on the first blank line in violet ink, and placed it in her card file, right behind Harold Dawson's card for the presumably lost Hardy Boys adventure.

"When you've finished this," Mrs. Peck said, "let's talk."

She smiled, then gestured toward the library door. Outside, Mott Simon still rooted through the flowerbed in the midday heat, streams of sweat pouring off his forehead. I don't know what he was doing, but he looked even more a mess than when I'd first seen him.

"Now, be careful out there, riding your bicycle along the road. It can be dangerous, with all those tourists headed for Sequoia, and the road being narrow."

"I know," I said, "I'll be careful."

Outside in the heat again, I mounted my bike, and pressed down on the pedals to get a jump on the ride uphill. Mott Simon looked up at me, holding a limp flower in his hand like one of the rag dolls I used to have. But he didn't say anything. I was grateful for that. He just looked at me, blinked, and then turned back to whatever it was he was doing in the dirt.

For a moment, I thought I heard the low rumble of thunder in the direction of the mountains. But it was probably just the motorcycles, farther up the canyon now.

The sun felt hot on my skin, and I squinted from the glare. Pumping as fast as I could, I reached the crest of the curve where the road wound through town. The breeze against my face felt cool and refreshing, a welcome relief from the oppressive heat.

It was very nearly noon, and I'd promised to meet my sister at the drive-in restaurant. Even though the town seemed sleepy, I remember I had the oddest feeling that things were about to change.

2. Robbers

As usual, Stephanie was late. I checked my watch to make sure it was ticking. Twelve o'clock turned into twelve-thirty, and still there was no sign of her. I was beginning to wonder if one of us had gotten the time or the place mixed up. I was pretty sure it wasn't me.

I swiveled around sharply when I heard old Mrs. Gregory burst into laughter. She and another Trailer Isle resident, Mr. Nickerson, were sitting on a bench near the water fountain. Mrs. Gregory didn't normally laugh – just pinched up her face into a smile – so I reached down to grab my notebook. It wasn't in my back pocket , so I made a mental note: Mr. Nickerson must be one heck of a joker.

I cased the drive-in restaurant for any potential suspicious activity. A few kids from Exeter High were hanging out around one of the umbrella-covered picnic tables, smoking cigarettes and trying to look cool. One of the girls wore a tie-dyed Tshirt that made her look like an accident victim.

Mr. Gruber, the owner, hurried through the double swinging doors into the kitchen, yelling something about fries and a shake.

Then I heard loud laughing, and it certainly wasn't staid, old Mrs. Gregory. It was two motorcycle riders, one a great big guy, the other one shorter, thinner. Their hair was almost as long as my hair, though my hair was certainly cleaner. They were wearing black leather jackets and black leather pants and black leather hats. All that leather! Didn't they know it was about a hundred degrees?

Were these the same guys who roared past the library? Or were there others? And why was Mrs. Peck so flustered by them, not wanting to answer my question?

I sure didn't like the look of those two guys.

There'd been a story in last week's paper about a robbery at The First National Bank. Two masked men had escaped on motorcycles. The crooks had eluded a dragnet of local police as well as the California Highway Patrol.

What if the two motorcycle guys I was looking at, right in front of me, drinking from the water fountain next to Mr. Nickerson and Mrs. Gregory, were the robbers? I couldn't believe my luck. If I captured them, I might win the reward the bank was giving out. I could use that money for college, or even to buy a new bike.

The smaller of the two motorcycle guys rubbed the back of his hand across his beard, then he looked my way. He stopped for a moment, then said something to his friend. I didn't think he saw me, but I couldn't be sure. What if he *had*? I crouched down lower.

When I looked out again from where I was hidden, I caught a glimpse of the little guy walking down the path to the left, then out of sight. Where was he going? Well, he did just drink an awful lot of water. Maybe he was...

Hold on! What was the big guy doing?

He was talking to Mrs. Gregory!

Mr. Nickerson and Mrs. Gregory obviously had no idea he was a wanted criminal. I should warn them.

But how? If I waved at them, they would wave back, being the nice folks they are, and then the big guy would turn around to see who they were waving at, and he'd see me half-hiding in the bushes, and of course he'd peg me in a minute.

I started to think about the little guy again, too. Where was he?

My mind flashed back to Mrs. Peck in the library. Was that why she'd been afraid to talk about them? She knew they were a band of marauding bank robbers, and was afraid of what might happen to a squealer.

Just then a hand clamped onto my shoulder and I jumped up off the ground like a rocket. The other motorcycle guy! I screamed, spinning around to fight him off, but the oak leaves slipped under my feet, like sheets of waxed paper, and in a flash I was lying dazed on my back looking up.

It was Stephanie.

"Don't *do* that," I said.

My sister just laughed.

"Steph, you scared me half out of my wits."

"Well, that doesn't leave you with much, then," she said. "What are you doing, anyway? Playing detective again?"

"Where were you?" I said, easing myself up. "You were supposed to be here an hour ago."

"Sorry," she said, "I was up at the candy store with the Pattersons and some of the other kids. I didn't realize it was so late. We were just having fun."

My heart was still pumping crazily. Stephanie looked passed me and waved to Mr. Nickerson and Mrs. Gregory, who were waving in our direction. I waved back. And the big motorcycle guy waved too.

"Here, turn around," Stephanie said. She picked at the back of my T-shirt, tossing oak leaves onto the ground at our feet. "It's a good thing I wasn't one of your crooks, or you'd be sprouting daisies right now, not oak leaves."

"There weren't supposed to be any crooks behind me," I said.

"There never are," Stephanie said. "Of course, that's when they get you." She cried out in mock pain, "Ah!" spinning around and pretending to have been shot in the back.

"Oh, stop making fun of me. Someday I'm going to solve some spectacular crime that will leave you all completely baffled."

Stephanie smiled. "You baffle me even now, sis." She squinched her face into a confused frown that made me giggle despite my best efforts not to. Then she smiled and ruffled my hair until it hung down over my eyes.

"At least you don't seem to have any trouble keeping busy around here," she said. "I wish I could say the same."

A chipmunk danced along the power line that ran from the pole by the road to the corner of the drive-in. If Stephanie hadn't been there I probably would have followed it to see where its nest was. But I didn't think she'd be interested. Frankly, there wasn't a lot in Three Rivers that *did* interest Stephanie. Come to think of it, the only things that ever interested her were clothes and boys.

"So where are Mike and Kathy?" I asked.

"At the swimming hole."

"Why not you then? You like to swim. And besides," I said, rolling my eyes dreamily, "Mike is there. You know, Mike, in swim trunks, swimming?"

"Very funny, Dani. I just don't like the swimming hole."

"Why? You always like swimming back home."

"That's different," she said. "That's a pool. Out here, there are tadpoles. I *hate* tadpoles."

"They're just around the edge, Steph. You've got to swim out a little bit, and then it's fine."

"I think I'll stick with pools," Stephanie said.

"Oh, come on. A swim would feel great right now. It's hot, and besides...I think the bank robbers have gotten away by now."

Stephanie sighed. "All right. I guess there's nothing better to do." She reached into her pocket and pulled out a slip of paper. "Here," she said.

"What's this?" I asked. I unfolded the paper like a piece of Japanese origami.

"It's a secret message," Stephanie said. "From headquarters."

"Let's see," I said, trying to decipher the scrawl. "Eggs, butter, milk, hot dog buns," I looked at my sister and laughed. "Must be in code, huh?"

"Yeah," Stephanie said. "And the code means, 'Pick up the groceries before Mom gets home, or it's liverwurst sandwiches again for dinner.'"

"Aye, aye, sir," I said. "Tell Agent Dad I'm right on it."

I picked up my bike from the dust, brushed off the streamers, and headed down the hill.

"Hey, Detective Deucer. What about our swim?" Stephanie yelled.

"Duty calls," I said. "I'll meet you later."

You never really understand a person until you consider things from his point of view—until you climb inside of his skin and walk around in it.

—*To Kill a Mockingbird* by Harper Lee

3. Accident

The world can be a surprising place sometimes. Strange things happen. You can't always depend on things to proceed in a logical fashion – which, come to think of it, could also be said of my sister Stephanie.

Okay, so maybe I'm not the world's deepest thinker. But I've been practicing my philosophy. All those old black-and-white detectives – Sherlock Holmes, Sam Spade, Perry Mason – always seem to know so much about the ways of the world. They know all about what goes on in the human heart, both the good and, unfortunately, the bad.

I'm not sure I understand all that myself – hey, I'm only twelve – but Mom says I have a way of listening to people that makes them enjoy talking to me. She says I have a sympathetic ear. I do think sometimes people sort of relax around me (Mom says it's my smile, but I don't think so), and they just open up to me, telling me things they might not tell somebody else. Anyway, I do like listening to people.

Well, *most* people.

Sometimes Stephanie wakes me up in the middle of the night to ask me questions like how we can know if we're really real or if we're just part of somebody else's dreams. (I just hope I'm not a part of Bobby Tollerude's dreams, that's all I can say.) Or she asks me how can we know that what we think we know is really what we actually know – and I just throw my stuffed gorilla at her and say, "Steph, will you please just shut up and go to sleep?"

I've never really believed in fate. I mean, it's so depressing to think our lives are programmed from birth, or even from before birth, and if I got the right issue of *TV Guide* I could look up what I'll be doing next Thursday, or who my boyfriend will be when I eventually have a boyfriend, which I'm sure I won't.

I choose to believe instead that I can control my own life. Stephanie may not always seem as if she can control hers, but I can control mine. At least when my parents let me.

Anyway, whoever was in charge of fate that day I bought the groceries was certainly having a fine time with me. Yessiree.

* * *

I bought all the stuff on my dad's list, plus a sack full of other things I knew we needed, and loaded it onto my bike. It was tough pedaling with all the extra weight of the groceries. Earlier in the summer, before we left L.A., I asked my parents to outfit my bike with a basket, or with saddlebags. They said they would, but it never got done. So I steered mostly with my hands gripped tightly near the center of the handlebars to keep the brown paper sacks centered between my legs. It was awkward.

The worst were the two heavy cartons of milk wedged inside one bag. I was worried that the condensation forming on the waxy cartons was soaking through the brown paper. I could feel the coolness of the milk cartons on the skin of my legs. Once – don't laugh – I looked down because I felt as if I'd had an accident.

There was also a head of cabbage squeezed in beside the milk (Mom was going to make coleslaw). It seemed on the verge of squirting out at any moment. Then I'd have to try and grab it, I thought, just like some porpoise jumping after a fish thrown high in the air. Ha!

Just then, the front wheel of the bike rode hard on the edge of the pavement where it met the shoulder of soft sand. It scared me. I thought I was going to lose my balance. I jerked the handlebars back toward the left and forced the tire up onto the pavement again. But then I nearly leaped out of my skin. A car horn blared right at my side. Where in the world did *that* come from?

My leg nearly ran up against the front fender, it was so close, and then I pulled back sharply toward the shoulder. The horn blared again loudly, and I swear I heard a man laughing.

The tires of the bike started to slide sideways on the sand of the shoulder, heading for the embankment. I looked back and caught a glimpse of an old banged-up white car which, unless I was seeing things, had no doors up front. It sped around the corner and out of sight. My bike careened down the rough grass hill toward a line of trees and a barbed-wire fence.

It all happened so fast. The bike hit a log and the front wheel jerked and I flew over the handlebars toward a tree that I hit with my shoulder or maybe my head and then I was lying on some rough stones wondering where the milk was and who was driving that car and why hadn't they stopped and was that blood I felt?

I don't really remember the impact. Luckily, I think my shoulder took the brunt of the force before my head clunked into the tree. The bike had crashed down onto my legs, taking a big gouge out of my right calf when the pedal hit me.

I wouldn't exactly say I blacked out. That would be a bit too dramatic. It was just so overwhelming, so dizzying and disorienting, I decided to lie still for a minute, to get my bearings.

Well, maybe it was a few minutes.

The next thing I remember, a hand was touching my shoulder. It reminded me of the way Mom sometimes wakes me for school.

I supposed the driver of the car came back to see how I was. Good. That would give me a chance to tell him what I thought of his driving.

I heard groaning. Had the driver been hurt too? But then I realized the groaning was coming from me.

For a moment, I saw no one. I just felt the kind hand on my shoulder. I could smell wildflowers, all around me – the wind must have shifted. They smelled... yellow.

"Are you all right?" said a voice.

It was a calm voice. It was also a voice I thought I'd heard before.

Like an idiot, I automatically replied, "Yes." That's when I started to feel the pain in my leg.

I should have screamed: *Of course I'm not all right, you idiot. I'm half-dead, wrapped around a tree, with a bicycle sticking out of me.*

But the bicycle was gone, and strong arms were carefully helping me turn over and face up out of the dirt. I leaned back against the smooth bark of the tree, and breathed in deeply. The scent of flowers was still there.

Pushing myself into a crouch, I carefully began to stand up. Actually, things didn't hurt as bad as I—

Ow! When I tried to put my weight on my right leg, a bolt of pain lanced through my calf, and I cried out. I probably would have fallen over if Mott hadn't caught my elbow.

Mott?

Of all the people in the world, why did it have to be Mott Simon who came to my rescue?

"You're bleeding," he said. He bent down to examine my calf.

"Is it bad?" I asked. I didn't want to look. My voice sounded funny, far away. Maybe I was in shock, I thought. I'd heard about shock in a first aid class at YMCA summer camp, but I wasn't really sure what it was.

Mott shook his head. "It's just a cut," he said. "But you should wash it."

I nodded. Mott took a step up the bank to where my bike rested on its side. I guess he'd laid it there after lifting it off me. He tipped it up and pulled it around to where I stood. We could both see the front wheel was so bent it wouldn't even rotate in the fork.

"Come on Dani, I'll help you," Mott said.

I smiled at him – well, I had to be nice, he *was* rescuing me, after all – and he grinned back crookedly. There was dirt on his cheek, and his hair was plastered to his head with sweat.

This was the first time I ever looked at Mott up close. Whenever our paths had crossed previously I tried to avoid him, keeping my eyes turned away so he wouldn't think I wanted to talk to him.

He looked older than my Dad did, but not quite as old as my Grandpa. Maybe in his fifties – I'm not good with ages.

His eyes were rimmed in red and were wide open and glistening. He hadn't shaved recently, and black and gray hairs were sprouting wildly all over his cheeks and neck. He hadn't bathed in a day or two either – I don't mean to seem rude or ungrateful for his help, but he was really smelly.

Mott lifted the front wheel of the bike from the ground, guided my right arm by the elbow, and steered me alongside the barbed wire fence. I thought we should be heading back up the embankment to the road – toward home – but I was still pretty dazed, and Mott seemed to know where he was going.

I'd only hobbled a few paces when I had a nasty thought. It was crazy for me to be letting Mott Simon lead me toward the woods. No one could see us from the road here. And the dusky sky was slowly starting to grow dark. I shouldn't be there, shouldn't be letting Mott Simon lead me deeper and deeper into the woods where we couldn't be seen and where no one could ever find me. My mother would kill me if she knew.

And yet, I felt safe. That's the strangest thing. I should have been scared out of my flip flops to be alone with Mott Simon, who everyone in town said was crazy. But as we walked along, I began to feel I couldn't have been in more secure company. There was just something about Mott I trusted, and I thought back to my conversation with Mrs. Peck in the library that morning.

We followed the fence for a hundred yards or so. Then, abruptly, Mott put his foot against one of the wooden uprights, and I saw several of the posts in this section were just hanging from the rusty wires, not going all the way to the ground. He pushed against the fence, and the posts flipped down, and without much difficulty I was able to step right over. Mott lifted my bike across and then hopped over himself.

It wasn't until we started walking through the closely packed trees and it grew darker as the sky was shut out overhead that I began to doubt my initial sense of safety. My face grew hot as I realized why: I just assumed Mott was leading me home; but if that was true, how did he know where I lived?

***

The woods began to thin and finally opened out into a wide field of dry grass spotted with big blackberry bushes. Mott pointed up ahead. There was a building at the other end of the field, a hulking half-wreck of sagging wood so weathered it was impossible to tell if it had ever been painted. It looked sort of like a barn, but with no farm nearby it looked sort of *not* like a barn too. It wasn't a house, though. Maybe some kind of storage place?

I looked around for other buildings, but saw nothing, not even remnants of concrete foundations jutting out of the long grass. Yet I sensed there *had* been more, and that this strange building was all that remained.

I could tell that Mott knew this place. We hadn't just stumbled upon it. Did Mott want me to see it?

He'd seemed nervous as we tramped through the trees, and I guess his nervousness rubbed off on me. But now he seemed relaxed and calm. I tried to feel the same, but this was just pretty weird.

He stood there, still and silent, just looking at the building, as if he unexpectedly stumbled upon a deer and was trying not to frighten it away.

When I glanced up at his face I realized his eyes were wet with tears. I guess he noticed me looking because then he said just one word: "Home." It was the first word he said since we started walking.

"You live here?" I asked. I was confused. I'd heard in town that Mott lived in a tacked-together shack under the bridge upriver, not in the woods.

Mott just kept walking ahead. The twisted frame of my bike was slung over his shoulder, partially hiding his face from view.

As we passed the building I stopped for a moment to peer through a crack in the boards that made up one of the walls. Inside it was dark and hard to see. There wasn't any furniture, though. Just a single room, empty from wall to wall.

"You live here?" I asked again. "This is your home?"

Mott put the bike down on the ground, wiped his forehead with his wrist, and looked at me.

"Used to," he said. "My ma and me."

"Your ma?"

Mott nodded, then picked up the bike again. He looked up. "I see the moon," he said.

It was true. It was getting pretty dark now. The moon shone brightly above the tops of the trees, and the sky was full of pinks and purples and grays, as if a fire burning beyond the hills was reflected high above us.

"Come on, Dani, we need to go now," Mott said.

I didn't want to go. I wanted to stay and talk to Mott and learn all about him and his mother. It never occurred to me he even *had* a mother – or a father or brothers or sisters or any relatives at all. It was hard to believe he'd ever been a baby, or a kid, or a teenager. It just seemed like he'd always been there, without beginning or end. I couldn't imagine him as anything other than the crazy man who lived under the bridge.

Mott walked halfway to the woods behind the house, or barn, or whatever it was, and he motioned to me again to follow. I was left looking into the dark emptiness inside the building, feeling the moon above me, and the gouge in my leg, which really started to smart now.

I followed him into the woods in silence, and soon I could hardly see in front of me. I made my way by listening to Mott and following his footsteps, watching the silhouette of his shoulders as he plodded through the underbrush. He must have known those woods well.

It seemed as if we walked for hours, although I know it wasn't really very far. I was just tired and my leg hurt, and all I wanted was to slip into my soft bed and go to sleep.

Then we stopped and I looked up and we were at the trailer park and Mott was laying my bicycle on the ground.

"Wash that cut, Dani," Mott said.

"I will," I said. I could hear my parents talking inside the trailer. Across the way, moths flitted in the lights above the shuffleboard court.

I knocked on the door, and when it opened my mother gasped and my father reached down to pull me up into his arms and into the trailer. The door shut.

"Wait," I said. "Mott."

My mother opened the door again, and we all three looked out into the night, but in the darkness beyond, Mott had disappeared.

That's when Mom saw the twisted bike at the foot of the steps.

"My God, Dani," she said. "What happened?"

4. Blackie

It took some fast talking to convince my parents that the accident was no big deal. At first it looked like the road to town was going to be off-limits for the rest of the summer, but when I assured them I'd just been careless and caught the front tire of the bike on the edge of the pavement (I sort of left out the part about the white car) they finally relented. Little good it did me, since the bike was completely out of commission.

Anyway, I decided my leg could use a little rest, and spent a couple of days reading part of the book Mrs. Peck had given me. It wasn't half bad.

Wednesday rolled around and my Dad made his weekly pilgrimage to Visalia for supplies and lunch with friends. Stephanie usually rode along, with some of the Patterson kids, so they could spend the afternoon at the mall. I'd rather shoot myself.

But this Wednesday found me squeezed into the front seat between Dad and Kathy Patterson so Mike Patterson and Stephanie could have the back seat to themselves. I'd tried putting my bent bicycle wheel between them, but they'd unceremoniously dumped it into the trunk.

After much protest, we stopped at the bike shop *before* the mall, where they said the wheel couldn't be fixed and it would be twenty-five dollars for a new one, thank you. Fortunately Dad didn't make me pay for it, since that was pretty nearly my life savings. Then I was sentenced to spend three hours at the mall, where

I entertained myself by browsing in the gift shops for handcuffs, which none of them had.

***

A week passed and I did some more reading and took it easy on my leg. Pretty soon it was good as new, and I was ready for some more detecting. The first place I thought of was Mott's barn.

It wasn't really a barn, but I called it that. Ever since he'd shown it to me I was fascinated by the place. But I wasn't quite sure it was safe to go exploring there. Not by myself, anyway.

So I took Stephanie with me.

It was about a halfmile downriver from Trailer Isle. We followed the river downstream, then cut through the woods in what I hoped was the right direction. By the river it was warm in the sun – hot, really – but in the woods it was cooler. I liked the shadowy stillness.

Half-hidden by the scrub oaks and giant blackberry bushes, the wooden building obviously hadn't been used in many years. A barbed wire fence encircled it, but it wasn't hard to squeeze through. We crossed a narrow patch of dirt and dried grass to get to the two large barn doors and swung one inward far enough to squeeze through, then let it close behind us.

It took a moment for our eyes to adjust to the dimness, but it wasn't really dark inside. The slatted walls and roof were gapped and knot-holed everywhere, and the entire side that faced the hot afternoon sun created a picket fence of light on the concrete floor. There were no windows and no other doors.

"Why do you suppose a barn would have a concrete floor?" Stephanie said.

I shrugged. "It's not a barn."

"Of course it's a barn. What else could it be?"

"I'm not sure. Maybe a revival house, or something."

"What's that?" Stephanie said. She was looking up into the rafters.

"A place where religious groups get together to sing and stuff."

Stephanie kicked up a layer of dust from the floor. The stripes of light cut through it as it swirled, creating a strange, undulating pattern in the air. "Nobody's gotten together to do anything in here for a while."

I pointed to the far end of the building. "But they did. Look. There's a stage."

A riser, about a foot high and ten feet square was centered at the far end, a few feet from the back wall. I walked over and examined it. The top and sides were covered in some dark color of carpeting, now laden with a thick layer of dust. Carefully I stepped up onto it. It felt like it had a wooden frame, with plywood under the carpet. It seemed pretty sturdy as I walked across it, then stepped back down to the floor.

Stephanie sighed. "Damn, I'm bored."

"Don't swear," I said. "It's low class."

"Who made you my keeper?" Stephanie said, kicking the stage with her tennis shoe. A cloud rose evenly across its surface, like a dust storm on some miniature planet.

"You wouldn't be bored if you had some interests," I said.

"I wouldn't be bored if the Pattersons hadn't gone into Visalia today."

"You've sure been spending a lot of time there. With all the neat stuff to do here, I would think you could find something better to do than sit inside a trailer all day talking about boys."

"We don't just talk about boys."

"OK, boys and clothes."

"You're certainly the high and mighty one, today. Anyway, don't talk to me about clothes. It just reminds me of that cashmere sweater I saw at Lerner's. I should have bought it when I had the chance."

"You couldn't buy it. You were broke, remember?"

Stephanie sighed. "There's no justice in this world. I'm the one who wants the clothes, and you're the one with all the money."

"I don't have *that* much money. And the reason I have any is because I don't spend it on cashmere sweaters," I said. I wiped the perspiration from my forehead. It was cooler in the barn than outside, but the air was heavy. "Anyway, I don't see how you can want a cashmere sweater when it's a hundred degrees out."

Stephanie plucked at the front of her T-shirt. "It's not for summer, it's part of the fall line. For when school starts up again."

I shook my head. "Summer vacation's short enough as it is. How can you be so anxious to get back to Los Angeles, and school?"

"Because I'm bored, that's how. You don't act like you're about to pass out from excitement either, you know."

"Well..."

"See? You're bored too," Stephanie said.

"OK, so today it's been kind of slow. But I am excited about one thing."

"Yeah? What?"

"I ordered this cool book I saw advertised in the back of *True Detective Magazine*. It's called *You Be The Detective*. It's all about modern criminal investigation techniques. It should be at the Kaweah post office any day now. I ordered it over a week ago."

Stephanie groaned. "And how much did this little gem cost you?"

Less than a cashmere sweater, I thought. "Ten dollars. Plus shipping."

Stephanie turned away, and paced off the distance to the far wall of the old barn. When she reached the wall she put up both hands and pressed against the boards. There was the creak of a nail moving. She quickly retracted her hands, and walked back to me. "Do you think this building is safe?" she asked.

I walked to one of the corner support posts, and prodded it gingerly with one hand. "It seems pretty solid. It's just the siding that's loose. I think the structure's sound."

"You talk just like Dad," Stephanie said.

"I'll take that as a compliment."

Stephanie shrugged. "Don't you ever find him a bit...dull?"

"I think a person has to make their own excitement," I said. *Now I sounded like my mother.*

"And how do you suggest we do that?" Stephanie said, mimicking her.

I shrugged. "Just...do stuff."

"What stuff?" Stephanie said. There was an old shovel leaning against the wall of the barn. She picked it up, examined the rusty blade, then set it tip down on the concrete floor and spun it, using her hand to keep the wooden shaft upright.

I shrugged. "I don't know. I just think we should take advantage of our surroundings. Shoot the rapids, maybe."

"We did that yesterday."

"It was the day before yesterday."

"Whatever. Anyway, I skinned my knee," Stephanie said.

"Geez, it's not like you broke your arm or something."

"That's next time."

"Very funny. Anyway, next time we should use air mattresses instead of inner tubes."

"Ouch!" Stephanie said. She let the shovel clatter to the floor, and examined her hand.

"Splinter?"

Stephanie moved so one of the bars of light slanting through the slatted wall fell across her hand. She worked her fingernails against the splinter, wincing. "What other great activities did you have in mind?"

"Why don't we ride into the library? You could get a book to read. It's a pretty good library, for a town this size. You should check it out." I smiled. "No pun intended."

Stephanie shrugged. Finished with the splinter, she crossed to the carpeted stage, and sat down.

I joined her. "The librarian – Mrs. Peck – gave me this neat book last week. I'm only about halfway through it, but it's really interesting. It's called *To Kill a Mockingbird*. It's about—"

"Since when have you been interested in hunting?"

"It's not about hunting. It's about this girl named Scout who—"

"Scout?"

"Yeah, and her brother Jem. They—"

"You're making this up."

"No, I'm not. Just listen a minute. There's a lot of stuff in this book that's relevant to what we're doing now."

"Relevant? To what? Sucking dust in an old barn?"

"Would you shut up and listen? At first Scout and Jem think their father is kind of a fuddy-duddy, because he's this sort of old-fashioned lawyer who believes in his principles. He's defending this Negro guy who's on trial for assaulting—"

"Black. They like to be called black, now."

"I know that. But this book takes place in the South, a while ago, I'm not sure when. Anyway, that's what they're called. Or worse."

"Worse?"

"Never mind. Anyway, Scout finds out their father is the best shot in town, because he kills this mad dog with one shot—"

"Charming."

"—and she comes to realize her father is risking his career to be defending this black guy, when everyone in the town believes he's guilty."

"Sort of like taking the summer off to write a book might be risky for an architect's career, huh?"

"That's not what's relevant about the book. I think Mrs. Peck gave it to me because there's this character in it named Boo Radley who's—"

"You *are* making this up."

"No I'm *not*." I punched Stephanie lightly in the arm. "Now just listen. When Mrs. Peck gave it to me, I was talking about Mott Simon – you know, the old guy who's always digging in the flower beds in town?"

Stephanie stopped rubbing her arm and nodded.

"Well, in the book, everyone thinks Boo is really weird, too. Maybe even dangerous. But Scout and Jem are really interested in him, and I think he's been leaving them little gifts in this tree, and I'm pretty sure they find out he's really nice, just shy, or maybe a little slow, or something."

Stephanie leaned back onto the stage and stared at the ceiling of the old barn. "You know, this doesn't sound like the kind of stuff you usually read. I thought you liked mystery stories."

I leaned back next to her. "It's not, I guess." There were shafts of light slanting through the gaps in the roof slats. One of them spotlighted a spider web high among the rafters. A fly struggled to free itself from the sticky netting. "Well, in a way it is. There is a mystery. I'm pretty sure the black guy's innocent, or Scout's father wouldn't be defending him. I mean, if he's guilty, there wouldn't be any point to the book, would there?"

Stephanie picked a burr off the front of her shirt and flicked it away. "Nope. I suppose not."

"So I'm pretty sure Scout's father gets him acquitted. But then the mystery is: who did it?"

"Boo."

"What?"

"Boo. The weird guy. He did it."

"Why do you say that?"

"You said he was weird. You said no one liked him, he might be dangerous. So he did it."

I sat up and brushed the dust from the backs of my arms. "I hadn't thought of that." Twisting my arm behind me, I began working on the back of my Tshirt. "I *hope* Boo didn't do it."

Stephanie sat up and looked at me. "Why? You just said he was weird."

"That's the point. That's why Mrs. Peck gave me the book." I stood up and brushed off the backs of my legs. "She wanted to show me that just because someone is different, it doesn't mean they aren't nice. And we should try to be nice back."

Stephanie stood up and swatted the dust from the seat of her shorts. "That's a crock." She coughed, and stepped out of the cloud of dust she'd created. "Anyway, you don't know anything about weird old Mott. For all *you* know he could be dangerous. Maybe Mrs. Peck meant you *should* be afraid of weird people if they're criminals. Mott could be hiding out from the law. You probably know more about this Boo guy than —"

Both of us turned at the sound of scraping outside the barn, near where we sat.

The scraping stopped.

I opened my mouth to speak, but Stephanie put her finger to her lips. We stood, waiting. The silence in the barn grew as we waited for the sound to repeat.

It didn't.

There was only the death struggle of the fly, high above.

A shadow moved across the slats, interrupting the piercing lines of sunlight, like a stick running along a picket fence. It moved the length of the barn, to where the twin doors stood closed, but unlatched. There was a rustling, and then the doors began to shiver.

Stephanie took a step back. Her heel bumped the edge of the stage and I grasped her arm to steady her.

One of the doors scraped open, and a black shape squeezed between, snuffling across the floor. Stephanie let out a squeal.

The shape hesitated. It was a dog, a black Labrador, its nose caked in dirt. Tongue out, its breath was heavy with the heat of the afternoon. Cautiously, it crossed the floor toward us, stopping just out of arm's reach. Then it lowered its stomach to the concrete floor and let out a long, low whine.

I reached my hand out but Stephanie pulled it back. "Leave it alone, Dani. You don't know anything about it."

"But he's friendly. Look at him."

"You know what Mom says about stray dogs."

"He's not a stray. He's got a collar." I crouched beside the dog, but it flinched away when I reached for the collar.

"Dani!" Stephanie said.

More slowly, I reached out and put my hand on the dog's head, then scratched him behind the ear. I rotated the collar until I could see the tag.

"His name's Blackie," I said softly, resuming my scratching.

"That's nice," Stephanie said. "Now leave him be, and let's get home."

The dog rolled over onto his back, offering up his stomach. I obliged by giving him a good belly scratch, using both hands.

Stephanie walked to the barn doors, giving the dog a wide berth. "Come on," she called. "It's almost time for Mom to get home."

I gave the dog a last ruffle and stood. Immediately Blackie flipped over and followed me to the door, panting. He paused while we stepped through, then cocked his head to one side. We were halfway to the fence surrounding the ramshackle structure when I looked back and saw him sitting in the doorway.

"Look, Stephanie. I think he's asking permission to follow us."

"No. Absolutely not. Come on. Let's get home."

"Coming," I said. But I turned back to the dog, and cocked my head in imitation. Blackie bounded across the barnyard. I stroked his back, then set off across the field after my sister, with Blackie close behind. Within a few strides, he was blazing the path, pausing to look back every few steps to make sure he was headed in the right direction.

"I swear, Dani, Mom is going to kill you if you bring that dog home," Stephanie said.

"I'm not bringing him home. He's bringing us home," I said. I passed my sister and leaped after Blackie, who scampered around me playfully.

Looking back, I saw Stephanie shake her head and then start across the field after us.

In a few minutes we came to the fence separating Trailer Isle from the fields to the east. I slipped under the bottom strand of barbed wire and Stephanie followed. Blackie was already on the other side, sniffing around the horseshoe pit.

It was mid-week, and the place was nearly empty. Only the Patterson's trailer and a couple of others were pulled up to the concrete pads that ringed the grassy loop.

"It looks like the Pattersons aren't back from Visalia yet," Stephanie said, as we crossed the grassy circle.

Blackie flushed a squirrel from among the oak leaves and acorns.

Even though we only had an eighteen-foot travel trailer it was in a nice spot, with a huge tree. Blackie scampered across the lawn and began snuffling under the picnic table beside the trailer. The car wasn't there – our mother wasn't home from her job at the Artist's Colony yet.

Before Stephanie and I got halfway across the lawn Blackie had vacuumed up the food in the dish we put out for Mrs. Gregory's cat , Tig.

"Hey!" yelled Stephanie. Blackie looked at her unrepentantly.

Our father's purloined 'Do Not Disturb' sign – a souvenir of a business trip to the Fresno Holiday Inn – still hung from the trailer's doorknob. Stephanie plunked down at the picnic table and busied herself rearranging the citronella candles we used to keep the bugs away. I washed out the cat dish using the hose while Blackie nosed around it, waiting for it to be refilled. He had to settle for water.

Dusk was gathering; the last rays of the afternoon angled up out of the oaks as the sun settled into the notch of the mountains to the west.

I turned away from petting Blackie when I heard the wheels of Mom's Lincoln on the gravel at the front of the trailer. She climbed out, collected her purse, slammed the door, and walked around the front of the car, then stopped when she saw the dog.

Stephanie spoke to the candles on the table. "I had nothing to do with it."

Mom arched her eyebrows, and looked at me expectantly.

"He's a stray," I said. "He followed us home." My mother's eyebrows went higher.

"He'd be good protection when I ride into town." *Oops. I shouldn't have said that.*

My mother shook her head. "Try again," she said.

"He could just stay with us a few days, until he finds his way home," I suggested. Mom's eyebrows narrowed. *That's even worse.*

"Well...He does have a tag..."

"Is it a county license tag?"

I bent and looked. Blackie licked my hand. "It has an ID number, and says Tulare County."

My mother nodded and looked at her watch. "First thing in the morning, you can call the county and find out where he belongs."

"Geez," I said, sitting down on the concrete slab with one arm around Blackie's neck. I ducked at the sound of the trailer door. It just missed my head, as Dad swung it open and stepped down onto the slab. Seeing me bent forward he said, "Oops. Sorry. Didn't know you were there." He turned to Mom. "Hi, honey. Hi, girls. Who's the dog?"

"A stray," answered Stephanie and my mother simultaneously.

"Blackie," I said.

5. Shack

My Mom hung up the phone. She tore off the top sheet from the notepad and handed it to me. "There you go. 48601 North Fork Road."

I looked at the paper. "Stegner?" I said. "What's that?"

"The owner's name," my mother said. "It sounded like some kind of fish, then Stegner."

Stephanie had been lounging on a bench in the trailer's dinette. Now she sat up. "Stegner? Karp Stegner?"

"That was it," Mom said. "Karp Stegner."

"Yuk," Stephanie said.

"Yuk, what?" I asked.

"That's Reba's father," Stephanie said. "You know, that redheaded girl who's always smoking behind the drive-in? The one who hangs out with those boys from Exeter High?"

"Oh," I said. I knew Stephanie despised Reba. She was the kind of girl our parents said came from the wrong side of the tracks. I'd seen her with several other kids hanging out around the candy shop one afternoon. They looked tough. Even when there were plenty of tourists around, I made it a point to avoid the place. But Stephanie liked one of the girls who worked behind the counter, June Tobler, so she spent a fair amount of time there.

"I know who Reba is," I said, "but I don't know her father."

"Oh yes you do," Stephanie said. "He's the one who drives that piece of junk with no front doors. You know her brother, too. He's that really weird little boy. We saw him at the drive-in restaurant last week. He was sitting on the bench in front, just rocking back and forth. Never says a word. At least not to anyone but himself."

I groaned. I felt sorry for Blackie, living with those people. I also felt sorry for myself, having to go there to return him. I stood up and stuffed the paper into the pocket of my cutoffs, then picked up the rope I'd found in the toolbox and turned to go.

"48601 must be about a mile up the river," called my mother, but I was already slamming the door.

Blackie wanted to bite the rope when I tried to tie it to his collar, but eventually he stood still and let me secure it. I led him to my bicycle and climbed on. Holding the rope against the handlebars, I carefully pushed off. "Come on, Blackie. Come, boy."

Between the trailer loop and North Fork Road, Blackie and I gradually got the hang of our new method of transit. After a couple of mishaps, Blackie learned to keep away from the front of the bicycle, and settled into an even pace beside me. I peddled casually, conscious of the dog's easy panting, and not wanting to exhaust him.

We passed the Clayton's house. Ray and Pearl Clayton were the owners of Trailer Isle, and lived in the only permanent home on the property. Flicker, an aging Palomino mare, grazed on the dry grass in the paddock across from the house. The first week we'd been at Trailer Isle, I asked Pearl Clayton if I could ride Flicker sometime, and Pearl had cautiously consented.

Under careful supervision she'd helped me with Flicker's tack and watched as we circled the pasture.

"You know your horses," Mrs. Clayton said when I came back and dismounted.

"Thank you," I said, patting Flicker on the neck as I led her back to the tack shed. "Two years of dressage classes taught me a lot. I'm going to miss them, this summer."

Mrs. Clayton watched me remove Flicker's saddle and begin to curry the horse's flank.

"What would you think about taking care of Flicker this summer," asked Mrs. Clayton. "Feeding and currying her every day, I mean. Ray and I are going to be away for a couple of weeks, and it would be a big help. If it works out, you could do it for the whole summer. In exchange, you could ride her whenever you liked."

"Really?" I asked. "That would be great. I'm very conscientious."

Mrs. Clayton nodded. "I can see that. I'm sure we can count on you."

And so I settled into a routine, caring for Flicker first thing after breakfast every morning. Sometimes I'd saddle her and take her for a ride around the pasture, using a downed tree trunk as a small jump. If I was feeling adventurous, I'd lead her out of the pasture and ride downriver, stopping below Slick Rock so the horse could wade out into the shallows for a drink before returning to the pasture.

Blackie darted in front of the bike and I ran over the rope, screeching to a stop. He waited impatiently for me to get him untangled, acting as if it were my fault, then hurried ahead as we got rolling again.

At the Trailer Isle entrance I checked carefully for traffic, then pulled my bike out onto North Fork Road heading upriver, away from town. I'd been up this way a mile or so, but I hadn't ever been as far as the Stegner's place. The road got pretty steep, particularly beyond the bridge.

The oak trees overhanging the road dappled it with millions of shadows that swam across my forearms, the bicycle, and Blackie. I was riding through a giant kaleidoscope, its patterns swirling around me in three dimensions. A split rail fence lined both sides. I passed a field of dry grass with cows grazing in it. On the other side of the field, beyond a grove of trees, there was a chicken ranch. I couldn't see it, but I could smell it.

There was an apple orchard on the left. My parents stopped to buy cider there on the first day we'd been in Three Rivers. Beyond the orchard was a three-car parking lot, and the Kaweah Post Office. I'd stop there later, after I dropped Blackie off, to check on my detective book, although I doubted it could have arrived yet.

The thought of books reminded me of my conversation with Mrs. Peck. On the way to the Stegner's trailer I'd have to cross the upper bridge where Mott lived *like some kind of troll*.

I hadn't been very nice to Mott. I felt bad about that. After he'd helped me all the way home the day of the bike accident, I hadn't even gotten a chance to thank him.

Maybe I should take Mrs. Peck's advice and try to make friends with Mott. He might be different, but he'd always been friendly to me when I'd seen him in town.

It is pretty weird to live under a bridge, though.

The road curved to the right. Up ahead the bridge crossed the North Fork of the Kaweah River. Beyond it the canyon narrowed and the river filled with rounded boulders piled at odd angles. Water bounded and sprayed over them, careening down the canyon.

Just before the bridge, on the near side, the pastureland terraced down to a wide sandy beach. It would have been a popular spot on the river except the water here was only a few feet deep and coursed rapidly over the boulders in its path. Mott had taken advantage of the gentle slope to create a colorful riot of terraced gardens. I didn't know much about flowers but I recognized pansies, carnations, zinnias, and poppies, and even several sunflowers over six feet tall. *He does have a way with flowers.*

Beneath the bridge Mott had used scraps of plywood to enclose a small shack, sheltered from both sides, but open to the river.

I pulled my bike off the road and leaned it against the bridge. Blackie nearly pulled me head first down the slope, but I yanked back on his rope. Letting him tow me along, I cautiously descended to the edge of the river.

"Hello?" I called.

The noise of the rapids was loud in my ears. I was hesitant to step under the bridge, even with Blackie along. "Hello?" Louder this time.

Something clattered inside the shack. A moment later Mott stuck his head out from behind the plywood wall. He cocked his head at me and smiled, then stepped onto the beach. He held a trowel in one hand and a flowerpot in the other. It was filled with tiny green shoots. "Hello," he said.

"Hello," I said again. Blackie stretched as far as the rope would allow, sniffing Mott's feet. I started to pull him back but Mott kneeled, and scratched him behind the ears. He talked to Blackie like a person, but I couldn't hear what he said. After a while Mott looked up and cocked his head to the side. *Just like Blackie would have done,* I thought.

I cleared my throat. "I, uh, I was..." What *was* I doing here, anyway? "I was passing by. To take Blackie home. I thought I'd stop and...say hello."

Mott nodded, continuing to scratch the dog. Blackie rolled over and offered his stomach.

"I, uh, also wanted to thank you," I added. "For helping me home the other day."

Mott nodded again.

"You have nice flowers," I continued, searching for a topic of conversation.

He smiled. "Thank you."

Not much of a conversationalist. "Do you live here alone?" I asked, although I knew he did.

But Mott surprised me by shaking his head. He rose, and Blackie immediately stood next to him. Mott motioned for me to follow, and stepped back into his shack. Hesitantly, I followed.

The inside of the shack was dark, but a quirk of the light caused the reflection of the ripples in the river to shimmer on the back wall, and my eyes quickly grew accustomed to the dimness. There was a bed, more of a pallet, really, with a neatly folded blanket and a pillow at one end. Gardening implements hung on one wall, neatly arranged from smallest to largest. There were spades, trowels, hoes, and some kind of weeder, plus several more tools I couldn't place. A plywood shelf held several cans of dirt. There were sprouts peeking from two of them. In the center of the shelf was a cylinder of mesh standing upright, with a piece of plywood on top. Mott pointed to it.

Bending to peer through the mesh, I saw the bottom was filled with dry grass. Three small, gray mice slept in a hollowed out depression.

"They're adorable," I said.

"My roommates," he said simply. Carefully he lifted the plywood cover from the mesh and set it across two of the cans. The largest of the mice opened its eyes and sniffed the air. Gently Mott scooped it up and set the sleepy creature in the open palm of his hand. It carefully explored the edges of its domain, sniffing the air. Mott plucked a sprout from one of the cans, shook the dirt from its roots, and offered it to the mouse, who eagerly took it and began nibbling, first on one end, then the other.

Tentatively I reached out a finger to stroke the tiny creature's head, but hesitated, looking at Mott for permission. He smiled and nodded. I touched the mouse gently between the ears, stroking my finger down its back.

"It's soft," I whispered.

Mott nodded. The mouse finished the sprout. Mott straightened his arm, and the animal scurried along it to his shoulder, exploring his T-shirt from neck to shoulder and back again. Soon it settled down to chew on the elastic neckband.

"Did you teach him that?" I asked.

Mott grinned. "Raised it. From a baby. I'm Hope's mother and father."

"Hope? Is that his name?"

Mott nodded. He motioned toward the cage. "Faith, Hope and Charity. A family. I rescued them."

"Rescued?"

Again Mott nodded. "I watched them since birth. They had a nest under the bridge, behind my wall. A big storm came this spring. The river washed into my house. It flooded their nest. They lost their mother."

Mott paused, and I could tell thinking about the mice losing their mother made him sad. When he continued, though, his voice was proud. "I rescued them. They've lived with me ever since."

"That was nice of you, Mott," I said.

He shrugged. "Everyone needs someone to take care of them, sometimes. My mice are good company." He looked out at the river. "Sometimes it's lonely here."

"How long have you lived here?" I asked.

"Ever since we got kicked out of home." The way he said the word home, he sounded like a small child.

"Home?" I said. "You mean that building you showed me in the woods? Did you live there?"

Mott nodded. "My Ma and me," he said. There was a longing in his voice, wistful maybe, like he was remembering better times. I wondered if he was sad, if his mother died and left him alone, or if maybe that was why he was so weird. Then I realized, of course his mother would be dead. Mott was no kid.

"Why were you kicked out?"

"It was a long time ago," he said, as if that somehow explained it.

I thought that was the end of the conversation, but then he said, "It was hard times. Nobody had any money. My ma used to do little things for people in town, and they'd give us food. She'd do errands, gardening, things like that."

I nodded. I guess that's where Mott learned about plants. He didn't seem scary when I pictured him as a boy.

"The man who owned the land let us stay in the tabernacle," Mott said.

Tabernacle? Is that what that barn-like thing was, or had been? And what was a tabernacle, anyway?

"He lived in a house near there." Mott said. I remembered glimpsing an old house off the main road in about that spot, but it looked overgrown and unused. "One day, they came and took away all his stuff, and boarded up the house. Bankers, my ma said they were, but they looked more like workmen."

Evicted, I thought. The bank foreclosed on the farmer who owned the land, maybe during the depression. Was Mott that old?

"When they found out where we lived, they made us leave, too."

I glanced from the mouse up to Mott. He looked so sad. "Where did you go?" I asked.

"Up here. To the bridge."

"To this shack?"

He shook his head. "I hadn't built it yet," he said. "There was a different bridge then, smaller. We slept on the sand."

I must have looked at him strangely, because he shrugged, and didn't say anything for a while. When he did speak, he said exactly what I was thinking. "It was cold," he said, and then he repeated the word "cold."

I tried to imagine what that must have been like, living under a bridge all winter, sleeping on the sand by the river. Is that what happened to his mother? Thrown out of her home because someone foreclosed on the owner? Had she died, living out in the elements? And if so, how did he manage to build a shack all by himself? How old was he?

I wanted to ask Mott all of those questions, but I found I couldn't. My throat sort of tightened up, and I wondered if I was going to cry. I suddenly felt really bad about what had happened to him. And when I thought about all of the mean things I'd said about him, I felt even worse.

Mott lifted the mouse gently from his shoulder and set it back into the nest. The other mice stirred and sniffed it, then jockeyed for space.

I suddenly had an almost overpowering urge to do something, anything, for Mott. Mrs. Peck was right. He *was* a nice man. Just different.

Blackie had wound his rope around my legs, trying to sniff at the mice, and now I disentangled myself. "I'm taking Blackie back home," I said. "To the Stegner's."

Mott flinched, and for a moment I thought something was hurting him. He sat down on the bed quite suddenly.

"Are you all right?" I asked.

His brow was creased, and his eyes had grown dark. "Stegner is a bad man. He's mean to animals. He hurts Blackie."

"How do you know?"

"I see him in town. He kicks Blackie. He kicks me, too, sometimes."

"Gosh." I didn't want to take Blackie home to someone who would hurt him. What would Mom say if I came home with Blackie and told her that I couldn't return him to an abusive owner?

But I knew what she'd say. The dog belongs to that man, and you can't keep it. I sighed. Maybe it was best to get it over with, before I got any more attached to him.

"Well, I'd better be going," I said. Blackie me followed me outside.

Mott followed, too. I climbed to the road he called, "Watch out for the sirens."

"Sirens?"

"All day, sirens, across the bridge. Lots of cars, a fire truck, a tow truck. Up the river. Be careful. Don't have another accident." He smiled at his little joke, and I felt myself smiling back.

"OK," I said. I climbed onto my bike and started across the bridge with Blackie leading the way. "Bye."

The road twisted steeply up the far side of the canyon, and I pumped with all my weight to keep the bike moving. There wasn't much on this side of the river. The terrain was too rugged. Stegner's was one of the few places up this far. I wondered if that was where the sirens had been headed.

6. Karp

The road narrowed beyond the bridge, and the grade increased. I rounded the bend and slid to a stop on the gravel.

Emergency vehicles blocked the road: a police car, a sheriff's car, an ambulance, a fire truck, and a tow truck, all with flashing lights painting the canyon walls in alternating stripes of red and yellow.

The tow truck had backed up to the edge of the turnout on the outside curve of the road. The operator stood near the rear, peering over the edge. The hoist cable disappeared into the canyon below. I pulled my bike up next to the sheriff's car, swung my leg off, and flipped down the kickstand. Still leading Blackie, I walked to the edge.

The canyon wall leveled off twenty feet below us, forming a flat terrace large enough for a small residence. Beyond that it descended steeply another 40 or 50 feet into the rocky river bed. The flat area showed signs of occupation: a washtub, a clothesline, a stack of old tires, a rusty pile of car parts.

The tow truck cable stretched over the edge of the turnout and across the terrace, suspending Karp's doorless car above the rocks. The slope was littered with wood, cloth, and metal fragments, most of them no larger than a seat cushion.

It looked as if someone had shredded a travel trailer using a Vegomatic.

Could there have been an explosion?

My eyes searched for the butane bottles I knew would have been fastened to the front of Karp's trailer. I saw one, half way down the slope. There might have been two, but I couldn't see another one. Still, there were no signs of charring or fire on the hillside. Wouldn't an explosion have started a fire?

Several officers watched from the edge of the road. The fire crew lounged on the steps of the fire truck.

Down below, a man emerged, feet first, from beneath the suspended car. He looked like a hospital orderly. He held a white sheet that flapped in the wind. Suddenly, Blackie's rope came out of my hand and the dog raced down the steep hillside and across the terrace toward the orderly. Before I could react, Blackie pushed his way past the man and started sniffing around beneath the sheet.

"Hey! Get out of there!" shouted the orderly. He reached for Blackie's rope, but drew back quickly when Blackie growled at him.

One of the policemen unsnapped the retainer on his gun holster.

"No!" I screamed, but I don't think he could hear me. I launched myself off the edge of the hillside without thinking, scrambling and falling down the slope. My momentum carried me past the orderly and I slid several feet before I could stop. Turning, I leaned forward and grabbed Blackie's rope, pulling him toward me. He came reluctantly, coughing against my tug. I shuddered at the sight beyond: a booted foot sticking out from under the sheet.

My pulse pounded in my ears. I turned away, hauling the dog after me. He resisted, but grudgingly followed as I struggled over the rocks back up to the road. A man in a sheriff's uniform reached down and helped me up the last few feet. I felt him studying me as I stood panting beside him.

"That was kind of a dangerous stunt," he said, not disapprovingly, I thought.

I nodded. Down below the orderly and another man maneuvered the sheet-draped stretcher up the hillside.

"That your dog?" asked the sheriff, nodding at Blackie.

I shook my head. The pair of boots still protruded from beneath the sheet. There were black web belts holding down the gruesome load.

A red car pulled into the turnout, and I held my breath while the dust floated past. A middle aged guy who had to be the fire chief leaned out the window and asked the sheriff, "What happened?"

"It looks like somebody pushed the car off the road. It went careening down the hill and slammed into the trailer. Smashed it all to pieces. As you can see, there's not much left."

Just then the men hoisted the stretcher over the edge of the turnout.

"The kids?" asked the fire chief softly.

The sheriff shook his head. "Apparently Karp Stegner was the only one unfortunate enough to be inside at the time. Never knew what hit him, I suspect."

The orderlies slid the sheet-covered stretcher into the back of the ambulance. One of the policemen stood at the edge of the road taking notes. The other supervised from the terrace as the tow truck driver engaged the hoist and dragged the car across the terrace and up toward the road.

"Are you sure someone did it on purpose?" asked the fire chief. "Couldn't it have been an accident?"

"Well, the emergency brake was released," said the sheriff. "Hard to figure how that could've happened accidentally. We'll know soon enough, though. After we've dusted for fingerprints."

The word fingerprints dragged my gaze away from the ambulance, and I studied the sheriff for the first time. He was a portly man, with a neatly trimmed gray mustache and soft blue eyes. His badge said Tulare County.

"When will you know?" I asked.

The sheriff seemed surprised. I guess he'd forgotten I was standing there. But he answered me. "Oh, usually takes two to three days to run the prints. Have to send them down to Visalia. If they don't come up with anything, the FBI can check national records. That usually takes a couple of weeks, though."

"May I come by to see you, in a couple of days? See if you know anything more?" I asked.

He cocked his head. "Did you know the deceased, miss?"

It was funny being called miss by someone old enough to be my grandfather. I shook my head. "No, not really. I've just seen him in town. I was bringing his dog back." I nodded at Blackie.

Blackie. What would I do with him now? Maybe my mother would have to let me keep him. Unless...

I looked up at the sheriff. "Do you know where Karp's family is now?" I asked.

"Staying with his sister, in town, I hear," the sheriff said. He pulled a small notepad and a stubby pencil from his pocket, flipped through the notepad, then licked the tip of the pencil and set it on the page. "May I have your name, miss? Just for my records."

I nodded. "It's Dani Deucer," I said proudly. *Wow, I'm a witness in a real murder case. Sort of.*

"Address?"

"My folks and I are staying at Trailer Isle for the summer. We're in number 14."

The Sheriff nodded. "Do you have a phone?"

"No. But you can reach me through the Claytons." Blackie twisted the rope around my legs, and I paused a moment to untangle myself. "I'd be happy to help, anyway I can," I added.

The sheriff smiled. "Why, thank you, miss. That's most gracious of you. If I have any more questions, I'll be sure to call. The Clayton's, that is."

I climbed onto my bike and let Blackie lead the way onto the road. I made a great show of looking both ways before the bike touched the pavement, wanting to be sure the sheriff saw how conscientious I was.

Maybe this summer won't turn out to be so boring, after all.

7. Sheriff

Before my mother was halfway out of the car that evening I was already trying to explain why Blackie was still there. Mom held up her hand. "I know, I know, word is all over town. I heard it at the art gallery. You weren't there when they...?"

I nodded.

"Oh, honey. How awful for you." She put her hand on my shoulder.

"No, Mom. It was neat. There were policemen, and an ambulance. They were hauling this car up with a tow truck. They had the body strapped to a stretcher —"

"Okay. Okay. We don't have to go into this right now. I'm sorry you had to see it."

"Well I'm not. It was really cool seeing the police in action. And the sheriff said he'd call me if he needed any help."

My mother looked at me as if I were from another planet. "Honey, a man is dead."

I dug the toe of my tennis shoe into the lawn. "Well..."

Mom shook her head. "You and your detective stuff. It's just a game to you. Think about how that poor man's children feel."

I sighed. Could she be right? I'd been so looking forward to playing detective. But I *had* been thinking only of myself. An image of my own father's foot sticking out from beneath the sheet on the stretcher flashed through my mind, and I shivered.

Mom opened the door of the trailer and stepped in. "Come on," she called over her shoulder. "Dad and Stephanie will be back from Visalia soon. Let's get some dinner started. You can help."

During dinner I described the crime scene in detail, more than once. Stephanie made an "icky" face when I talked about Karp's boot sticking out from under the sheet, and my mother told me to skip the gory details. I also mentioned my visit to Mott's shack.

"I think you should stay away from him, honey, " Dad said. "It's not normal to live under a bridge."

"But Mrs. Peck says—"

"Mrs. Peck isn't your parent. It's all well and good to show consideration for those who are different from us; that doesn't mean we need to put ourselves in danger just to be nice."

Mom said, "You think Mott is dangerous?"

Dad set his fork down and wiped his mouth with his napkin. "I'm not saying he's dangerous. I'm just saying that we don't know him. It's better to be safe than sorry."

"But Dad," I said, "You should have seen how gentle he was with Blackie—"

"Speaking of Blackie," Mom said, "Tomorrow you need to call the sheriff and find out exactly where Karp's family is staying. I'm sure they're worried about the dog, and in their time of sadness having him around would no doubt make them all feel better."

I nodded. I'd expected it, but I'd been avoiding the subject, hoping that somehow the dog would get overlooked and end up mine by default. This wasn't turning out the way I'd hoped.

***

I got up early the next morning. I'd planned to spend the day playing with Blackie, then return him. But the more I thought of the Stegner kids pining for their lost dog, the more guilty I felt. So before the sun was even on the valley floor I headed out of Trailer Isle on my bicycle with Blackie alongside.

When I got to North Fork road I impulsively turned right. In spite of what my father said I knew Mott wasn't dangerous. And I was sure he'd enjoy seeing the dog again.

The air had a crisp bite to it as I pedaled up to the bridge. It never really got cool in the evenings this time of year, but before the sun hit the road it wasn't so blisteringly hot, and I enjoyed the feel of the wind on my face. I propped my bike on its kickstand at the top of the grade and scrambled down beside the bridge, with Blackie leading the way.

"Mott," I called.

There was no reply. Just the babble of the river beneath the bridge.

I peered into the shack, letting my eyes grow accustomed to the dim light. The bedding was rumpled, and his pillow lay on the ground. Several of the gardening tools had been knocked from the wall and lay in a heap. The lid of the mouse cage had also been knocked askew.

What happened here? The whole thing was starting to creep me out. I thought of my father's warning. Did Mott do this?

I looked up and down the river, but there was no sign of anyone. Cautiously I stepped into the shack and peered into the mouse cage. All three mice were still there, asleep in the middle of their straw bed. Their water dish was empty, and there was only bedding in their food dish. Carefully I removed the lid and lifted the two dishes from the cage. I refilled the water dish from the river, and transferred a handful of grass seed from a bag on the bench into the food dish. Replacing both dishes, I carefully realigned the lid.

It didn't seem like Mott to leave such a mess. Where was he?

Maybe he headed into town early this morning and some kids had come by and messed up his place. I'd try to find him in town and tell him.

I climbed back onto my bike and headed downriver. Something about that explanation bothered me. I was halfway to town before I realized that Mott would have fed the mice.

***

The sheriff was walking back from the impound yard behind Pat O'Connell's gas station when I pulled up in front of his office. I could see Karp Stegner's car in the junkyard out back. The hood was smashed in, and the windshield was broken. There was surprisingly little other damage, considering the plunge it had taken and the condition of the trailer it had demolished.

By the time I finished tying Blackie to one of the awning posts in front of the office the sheriff had reached the porch. He held the door open for me as I stepped into the small waiting area. The door banged behind us and he tossed an envelope onto the unoccupied receptionist's desk.

"Good morning, Miss Deucer. What brings you into town so bright and early?" he said.

"I need to find out where the Stegner kids are staying, so I can take Blackie back."

"They're staying with Miss Stegner, Karp's sister. She has an apartment behind the market. You know, about a block up on the other side of the highway?"

I nodded. The Three Rivers Market was my second most common destination in town, after the library. I was particularly fond of the orange Dreamcicles in the ice cream case. I turned and rested my hand on the doorknob. "Well, I guess I better be getting him back, then."

"You don't seem very anxious to return him."

"No. I'd love to keep him. But Mom says no. I'm sure the Stegner kids will be happy to see him."

The sheriff grunted.

"Any more news on the murder?" I asked.

He leaned against the receptionist's desk and stuffed his hands into his pockets. "You're quite the investigative reporter, aren't you?"

I tossed my hair off my forehead. "My friends all say I'm going to be a detective."

"A very honorable profession," the sheriff said. "If not a high-paying one."

"I'm more interested in seeing justice done, than in making a lot of money," I said.

"Well, then you'll be happy this case got wrapped up so quickly."

I leaned forward conspiratorially. "Already? What did you find out?"

"The crime lab in Visalia called me at home this morning before I was even awake. The fingerprints on the steering wheel popped up with an early match. The perp had a prior conviction for vagrancy in Visalia, so they had him on file right there."

"Perp?"

"Sorry. Perpetrator. Cop talk."

I nodded. I should have known that from TV.

The sheriff yawned. "Anyway I got up with the chickens, and already made the arrest. He's down in the jail behind the Visalia police station right now."

"Wow. That *was* fast." It was almost thirty miles to Visalia. The sheriff must have gotten up *really* early.

"Yup. Sometimes we get lucky and everything falls into place."

"Was it somebody who had a grudge against Karp?"

He nodded. "They almost came to blows just last week. Several witnesses. Looks like a slam dunk case."

"So he lived in Visalia?"

"No. Local guy," the sheriff said. "Lives right up the North Fork."

I felt my blood go cold.

"Name of Mott Simon," continued the sheriff. "Sort of a bum. Squatter lived under a bridge, if you can imagine."

"No," I said softly. There was a chair by the door. I sat down in it, hard.

"No?"

"Not Mott. He couldn't have. He's so kind. So gentle."

"You know him?"

"I was just at his place yesterday. He's just a nice old guy who wouldn't hurt anyone."

"That's not what Mr. Gruber over at the drive-in says. Mott and Karp just about got into a fistfight last week. And his fingerprints were all over the car. Especially the steering wheel. So it's pretty clear he did it."

I shook my head, but I didn't know what to say. It couldn't be true. The way Mott acted yesterday, I was sure he didn't know why all those emergency vehicles had gone up North Fork road. Unless he was hoping to use me as an alibi...

I was going to tell the sheriff about my visit to Mott, but the telephone rang. He picked it up, grunted once disinterestedly, and then a second time as his eyes widened. "Be right there," he said and dropped the receiver back onto its cradle. He brushed past me, strode to the door, and opened it.

"Sheriff—" I began.

"Got to go. We'll talk later. There's a fire behind the drive-in."

He was in his car and backing out onto the highway before I'd cleared the bottom step. A fire engine's siren wailed in the distance.

A half-mile up the highway there was smoke rising between the trees.

8. Fire

The smell of smoke was strong in the air as I pedaled up the highway toward the Three Rivers Market. I pulled my bike behind the building and parked it near the corner. Some wooden steps led to a walkway that ran the length of the structure, with several apartments opening onto it. A group of residents stood at one end, craning their necks to see the billowing smoke.

I started for the steps when I heard a voice call out, "Reba!" A redheaded woman in a floral print housedress leaned against the railing. Her hair was in curlers, and a cigarette dangled from her lips. She called to the girl who was just rounding the far end of the building, coming from the direction of the smoke. "Reba, what's all that smoke?"

"I dunno, Auntie. Something's on fire."

"I can see that, child. You think I'm daft or something? Get over here and see if you can find Ardy. He's disappeared again." The woman turned and said something to the man next to her. He nodded. He was wearing a black leather jacket. A biker, I thought. And indeed there was a motorcycle, a big Harley Davidson, parked near the bottom of the steps.

Reba started to go in, but I called to her. "Reba?"

She turned to face me, one foot on the step. She was slim, with red hair like her aunt, and a smattering of freckles across her nose and cheeks. The left knee of her jeans was torn, and her sandaled feet were dirty.

Dark circles underlined her bloodshot eyes. I wondered if she'd been crying or was just tired.

"Who're you?" she asked. Then she saw the dog.

"Blackie," she said.

Blackie was standing next to my leg, but when Reba turned and knelt he walked over to her and pushed his nose into her outstretched hand. She flinched as if he'd hurt her. She extended her other hand and petted him on the head. He wagged his tail.

"I brought him back," I said simply.

Reba looked up. "Oh." She turned to look toward the walkway. Some of the neighbors still stood at the railing, but her aunt had gone in. Reba shook her head. "Irene won't let us keep him."

"Irene?"

"My aunt. She said if he showed up we had to take him to the pound. The apartment don't allow no dogs." She turned her attention back to Blackie, scratching him behind the ears. "Oh Blackie, I'm so glad you're all right, boy. I was afraid that car got you just like it got Pa. Ardy said you wasn't there, but he makes stuff up."

My heart did a flip-flop. Surely my mother couldn't expect me to give Blackie back to Reba if that meant Blackie would end up at the pound. Maybe there was still a chance of talking Mom into letting me keep him. Still, he belonged to Reba. But if I could talk Reba into letting me have him...

"I found him a couple of days ago," I said. "Well, actually he found me. He'd wandered about a mile downriver from where the accident—"

Reba looked up with a start, and I was immediately sorry I'd mentioned the accident. But she smiled and said, "Must've scared the stew out of poor old Blackie, that big old crash. Geez, it must've been one loud noise."

"You weren't there? When it happened, I mean?"

"Nope. I was here in town. I walk down most afternoons, and then Irene drives me home when she gets off work."

"You walk all the way into town?"

Reba shrugged and gave me a look that said mind your own business. It was an awfully long walk into town from Karp's place, maybe five miles.

"So you and Irene found the wreck?" I asked, trying not to sound as interested as I was.

Reba nodded. "Ardy was there, but no sign of Karp. It was too dark to see anything, The next afternoon they found him. So Irene says I'm livin' with her, now." Reba stood up and wiped her hands on her jeans.

For someone whose dad just got killed she doesn't seem very upset, I thought. *I wonder if she's even telling the truth.*

"Here, you wanna see something?" asked Reba. I nodded. Reba reached for Blackie's rope. Reluctantly, I handed it to her. She squatted to unfasten it from his collar.

Once the rope was loose, she ruffled his fur and began playfully calling to him. "Come on, boy. Come on. Wanna play tug-of-war? Get the rope, Blackie. Get the rope." She lashed the rope on the ground in front of the dog, and he seized it and began tugging. Caught by surprise in spite of herself, Reba almost toppled forward before she managed to regain her balance. She dragged Blackie back a few feet, but the dog redoubled his efforts, and again Reba was pulled forward, nearly off balance.

Now Blackie was jumping side to side, and Reba was getting tossed back and forth, laughing and trying to win back some of the rope. But Blackie was too strong for her, and in a moment he yanked the rope out of her hand, and stood triumphantly shaking it, eyeing her.

I found myself laughing, too. "One thing's for sure," I said. "Blackie sure does know the ropes!"

Reba laughed and handed me the rope. "I taught him that myself, when he was just a puppy. He's really good at anything to do with rope. Tugging, chewing, I even saw him work a knot loose once, on our old tire swing."

Reba didn't seem so bad, even if Stephanie didn't like her. She certainly seemed fond of Blackie. She wouldn't really let Blackie go to the pound, would she?

I stuck out my hand. "I'm Dani, by the way."

Reba reached out and we shook hands. "Reba," she said. "But you knew that."

I nodded. She sort of grimaced when we shook, which seemed odd, because I didn't squeeze all *that* hard. There was something weird, sort of guilty seeming, about Reba. I had to remind myself I wasn't here about her, but about Blackie.

"You, ummm... you wouldn't really let Blackie go to the pound, would you?" I asked.

"*I* wouldn't," Reba said. "But Irene says—"

Reba had turned to gesture toward the apartment. Now she stopped speaking, as if she saw something. At first I couldn't tell what she was looking at. But then I noticed something moving in the shadow of the steps. It was a small boy.

"Ardy. Come out of there, right now," Reba said.

Slowly the boy emerged into the sunlight. His skin was pale, and he wore baggy, nondescript clothes. A shock of brown hair covered one eye. He was looking at Blackie.

"You know Auntie told you to stay inside, Ardy. What are you doing out here?"

Ardy shrugged. Blackie went up to him and sniffed his shoes, then waited to be petted. Ardy obliged.

"Blackie's the only dog Ardy isn't afraid of," Reba said. She watched her brother pet the dog for a minute. "Poor Ardy. As if he didn't have enough problems already."

Her brother seemed oblivious to her comments. "What do you mean?" I asked.

"Ardy's autistic. That means he doesn't really connect with the world, the way the rest of us do. Some days are better than others. Usually he'll talk to *me*, at least." She sighed. "But I don't think he's said a single word since the trailer went over."

"He was there?"

"Yup. It's really tweaked him. He's been sneaking around like a little mouse, ever since. Sheriff came by to talk to us and all Ardy would do was shake his head, over and over."

"It must've been pretty awful for him to see your dad get killed," I said.

Reba shrugged. "I suppose. Frankly, Irene's a lot easier to live with."

As if on cue, the door to the apartment opened and Irene leaned out. "Reba!" she called. "I said to come find Ardy!" Then the woman saw him. "Ardy, I told you to stay in this apartment. Get in here. Now!"

Ardy turned, robot-like, and marched up the steps. Irene watched him until he stepped past her into the apartment, then turned her attention back to us. "Reba! Is that your dog?"

Reba glanced at me, but I didn't know what to say. She turned back to her aunt. "No, ma'am," she called. "Not anymore. He's got a new home now."

"Well thank goodness for that," her aunt said. "Now get in here and take care of your brother. I've got to get to work, and I can't be expected to keep track of that boy all day long."

As Reba climbed the steps, she turned and gave me a wink.

9. Nick

I still couldn't believe my luck. It was almost too easy. When I told Mom the Stegners had threatened to take Blackie to the pound, she said I could keep him.

Now that a few days had passed, some of the initial elation was wearing off, but I still found myself amazed that I had my own dog. I'd quickly fallen into a routine of feeding and watering him first thing in the morning. Then together, we headed for a before-breakfast dip in the swimming hole.

Blackie had a knack for retrieving things thrown into the water. I'd toss sticks, and old tennis balls, or even my beach towel as far out into the swimming hole as I could. He'd plunge in and retrieve them, showering me each time with a spray of water as he shook himself dry.

And of course he was fond of rope. Any stray rope lying about was fair game. Blackie would grab the end and tug on it, worrying it until it frayed or came loose, then drag it about trying to coax me into another game of tug-of-war.

On a walk downriver from the swimming hole we'd come upon an old suspension bridge: two cables with wooden slats fastened between them. It crossed the river a few feet above the high-water mark. Parallel ropes acted as a crude railing to help pedestrians keep their balance on the swaying bridge. The railing ropes were anchored to the suspension cables with dozens of vertical ropes that were individually knotted between cable and railing.

Before I even finished climbing up the riverbank at the near end of the bridge, Blackie was halfway across, worrying the loose end of one of the vertical ropes. He looked a bit like a giant black fish, struggling at the end of a fishing line.

By the time I reached him, he'd managed to free the top end of the rope from the railing, and was proudly prancing across the bridge with it dragging behind.

Each day after breakfast, I went out to feed and curry Flicker. The horse was always glad to see me, not least because I often took a sugar cube from the bowl on the kitchen table. When I'd finished forking hay into the crib beside the tack shed, I usually headed back to our trailer for a tall glass of water. Even that early in the morning the pasture was already heating up, and the hay dust was dry in my throat.

When I'd cooled off I rode my bicycle upriver to feed Mott's mice, then stopped at the Kaweah Post office to see if my book about detecting had arrived. At first, I took Blackie with me on these forays, but after a few days I began to notice him lagging behind as I rode my bicycle. I stopped by the side of the road and waited for him to catch up. He seemed to be limping.

I gently lifted a front paw. It looked red and when I tried to touch it Blackie jerked away. I examined the other front paw and found it was the same.

"Oh, Blackie," I said. "Has all of this running on pavement been too hard on your poor feet?" I scratched him behind one ear and he panted happily at me. "I'm sorry, boy. I should have realized." I pedaled slowly home and left him tied contentedly in the shade of the picnic table while I rode back to the post office.

The Kaweah Post Office is one of the smallest post offices in the country. It's little more than a shed with a porch, constructed entirely of rough-hewn lumber, unfinished except for the white lettering on the sign above the porch. Inside, there's a single room, about five feet square, with a window that opens into an even smaller space where the postmistress works. One wall is covered with post boxes, each with a small bronze door adorned with elaborate filigree. Standing in the middle of the room I could touch all four walls by simply lifting my arms.

I'd checked my box each day for two weeks, ever since I'd ordered the detective book, with no luck. But today, when I opened the brass door, I found a curled manila envelope. Anxiously I struggled until I finally managed to bend and extract it through the small doorway. I tore it open and removed a small pamphlet. *You Be The Detective*, read the cover.

Hmm. This looked more impressive in the ad...

I flipped through the pages, noting the headings: *Physical Evidence: Leave No Stone Unturned, The Investigative Process: Interviewing Witnesses, Putting Together the Case: A Matter of Justice.*

Well, this looks pretty good. Short, but good.

I settled myself onto the dusty front step and began to read.

An hour later the shadow of the post office had slid across the steps, and I was just closing the pamphlet as a car pulled into the three-car parking lot. Nick Nickerson, one of our neighbors from Trailer Isle, climbed out. Nick was a burly man in his sixties who always reminded me of Mr. Wilson, in the Dennis the

Menace cartoons, but with a friendlier disposition. He slammed the door of his dusty old sedan and walked around it, shuffling a handful of letters.

"Good morning, Mr. Nickerson," I said.

He smiled when he saw me. "Good morning, Dani. Reading your mail?"

"That's for sure! A whole book. Well, more of a pamphlet, really."

"What's it about?"

"Being a detective. The investigative process, stuff like that."

"Hmm. Sort of odd reading material for a young lady, isn't it?"

"Not for me," I said. "That's about all I ever read."

"Why the interest in detecting? Not much call for that around here, I wouldn't think."

I got to my feet and Nick stepped up onto the porch next to me.

"Oh, you might be surprised," I said. "We're smack dab in the middle of a murder mystery right now, in fact." I handed him the book.

With some difficulty he tucked his letters into a shirt pocket, leaned against the porch railing and flipped absently through it. "Really? What's that?"

"Karp Stegner," I said.

Nick stopped flipping and looked at me. "I thought that bum killed him."

"Mott's not a bum," I said.

"If he isn't a bum, I don't know what one is. Or is he really an eccentric millionaire who just happens to like living under a bridge?"

"He may be eccentric, but he isn't a bum. He's very nice. And he didn't kill Karp Stegner."

"That's not what I've heard around town."

"From whom?"

"Well, Phil Gruber, for one."

"Who—? Oh, yeah, the drive-in guy."

Nick nodded. "Yep. Gruber says Mott and Karp got into a scuffle the day before Karp was murdered. Says he heard Mott threaten to kill him."

"He probably made Mott mad. Karp wasn't very nice, you know. But there's no way that kind old man could've killed anyone."

Nick shrugged. "Well, if you can prove that, you are one super detective." He handed the book back. "Personally, I think you should be a little more discriminating in your choice of clients." He turned to go into the post office.

"How so?" I asked.

"Next time, pick one who can pay you," laughed Nick, as he stepped into the building.

I scuffed my heels over to my bicycle and climbed on.

It's not a matter of money, I thought. It's a matter of justice. People are just too quick to believe what they want.

I turned my bike toward Trailer Isle, then stopped before the tires even hit the pavement.

How could I prove Mott was innocent? I'd just finished reading a book about detecting. Maybe it was time to put some of its advice to work. What had it said? *Physical Evidence: Leave No Stone Unturned.* That's what I'd do. I'd examine the crime scene.

I pulled my bike onto the road and headed upriver.

When I got there I found yellow tape along the turnout, cordoning it off. 'Police Line – Do Not Cross,' it read. I sighed. Peering down the slope I could see the litter of debris from the demolished trailer, little changed from my previous visit. There were deep gouges in the hillside where the car was hauled back up by the tow-truck.

Physical Evidence: Leave No Stone Unturned. These stones have already been pretty thoroughly turned, I thought. Where would I start if I dared to cross the line? I had no idea. It wasn't like there was a murder weapon I could find. Everyone knew Karp was killed by the car. And Mott's fingerprints were on the car. That didn't look good. I sighed again.

Hmmm. *The Investigative Process: Interviewing Witnesses.* Maybe I should start with people. I'd already talked to Reba. She'd seemed nice, in spite of what Stephanie said. And she wasn't there when it happened. At least that's what she claimed. Presumably she had friends in town to back up her alibi.

What about Ardy? He'd been there. And Ardy was pretty weird. In fact, I found myself feeling a little scared of him. That's silly, I thought. Just because he's different, doesn't mean I need to be scared of him.

Ardy had clearly been traumatized by the accident. Maybe he'd driven the car off the edge. Did he even know how to drive?

Reba said Ardy usually talked to her. Had he talked to her about the accident? Was she just covering for him by claiming he hadn't? Obviously Reba hadn't been very fond of their father. Maybe she put Ardy up to it, promising him that she wouldn't tell...

So many theories, so little evidence. Where to start? Were there any witnesses I hadn't already talked to?

There was one. I turned my bike downriver and let the grade carry me toward the Three Rivers Drive-In Restaurant.

10. Fight

The Three Rivers Drive-In Restaurant was a long, low building with wooden siding. Out front were a half dozen parking spaces where patrons could pull up and be served by a waitress who spent the day padding between the cars and the walk-up window. Those wishing to get out of the sun could sit at one of the three picnic tables inside, where the swamp cooler on the roof waged a losing battle with the summer heat.

I pulled my bike around to the back. It was the restroom building that burned to the ground. Mr. Gruber was out there, throwing charred boards into the restaurant dumpster. He was a short, pudgy man with a bushy black mustache that he chewed on when he was thinking. His plaid shirt fluttered from the top of the chain link fence by the dumpster, and his bare chest was drenched in perspiration and glistened in the hot sun. He seemed grateful for the interruption when I asked if I could talk to him about Mott.

He stepped through the back door to the kitchen and emerged a moment later with two bottles of Coke. Handing one to me, he sat on the low concrete block wall and downed half of his bottle in a single long gulp.

"Yeah, I used to give old Mott a free burger now and then," he said. "In return, he'd keep my planters out front of the drive-in weeded. Did it better than that worthless gardener I used to pay too much money for nothing. Old Mott, he'd plant new flowers in the spring, sometimes in the fall too. Started 'em in his own garden, then brought 'em out here in egg cartons and put 'em in. Kept the grass out of the beds. Always looked real nice."

Mr. Gruber took another gulp from his Coke bottle. "Hard to believe old Mott's a murderer. Seemed such a gentle sort. 'Course, who knows what's goin' on in that crazy head of his? Just glad it wasn't *me* he did in. The missus'd miss me... I hope."

I took a sip of my Coke and sat on the wall next to him, trying to decide how to get Mr. Gruber to have the same conversation with me he'd had with Nick. If I asked him outright, would he just tell me? Somehow I doubted it. So I asked the obvious question. "Do you really think Mott killed Mr. Stegner?"

Mr. Gruber shrugged. "I suppose," he said. "Anyways, not many around here'll miss Karp Stegner."

"If that's so, isn't it just as likely someone else killed him, then?"

Mr. Gruber shook his head. "Karp used to tease Mott somethin' fierce. Why, even on the day before the murder I heard Karp and Mott going at it."

"Going at it?"

"I guess Karp wanted to pull his car into the parking space out there by the planters. Mott was kneeling there, working on the planter when Karp pulled up."

"How did you happen to see this?" I asked. Mr. Gruber gave me a funny look, like I was suspicious of him, or something. I guess it was kind of a tactless question, but he answered me anyway.

"Karp laid on his horn, which caught my attention from where I was working the outside counter. I thought old Mott would jump out of his skin when that horn went off right behind him. And Karp just kept comin'. I was sure he was goin' to drive right over Mott's legs, but that old guy's pretty spry. He scrambled out of the way, but he didn't have time to save his egg cartons of flowers. Karp drove right over 'em – on purpose, too."

"That wasn't very nice." It was all I could think to say. I hoped he'd go on without me asking any more dumb questions.

Mr. Gruber sniffed and wiped his arm across his mouth. "When Karp got out of the car, he kicked one of the smashed cartons over to Mott, and told him he should have a gardener's truck, or a car or something for his stuff, if he was gonna have his own business."

"Do you remember anything he said?"

Mr. Gruber scrunched up his face and said, "Not really." And then, "Well, it went something like, 'Mott, you need yourself a car. Then you could have your own business, like me.' Stuff like that, teasin' him, sort of. Tellin' him he could be a travellin' gardener, goin' around town prunin' peoples' hedges, and such."

"What did Mott say?"

"Nothin'. He just sat there on the pavement by the planters, lookin' at Karp, real sad, like. Even when Karp asked him if he could drive a car, or if he was too stupid, Mott didn't say a word. I think that made Karp mad, that he couldn't get a rise out of him. He started shouting at Mott, accusing him of bein' rude to him."

His Coke was gone, and Mr. Gruber eyed the empty bottle wistfully, as if wishing it would magically refill itself. I figured he was done with his story, and I was just starting to slide off the wall when he said, "About that time Karp caught sight of that Labrador dog of his – the one I've seen you goin' around with. The dog was sniffin' around the crushed flowers Karp had kicked over to Mott. I guess the lab jumped out of the car when the kids – you know, Karp's son and daughter – got out and came into the restaurant. Mott started pattin' the dog, and Karp really blew his stack. 'Blackie! Get over here!' he screamed. Then he screamed at Mott, too. 'You leave that dog alone, Mott, you hear? That dog likes people too much as it is. He'll never grow up to be a guard dog if he don't get treated like one, if he don't learn to mistrust strangers.'"

What a jerk, I thought. But I wanted to keep Mr. Gruber talking about that day, and not go off about Karp, so I said, "What did Karp do?"

"He walked over and kicked that poor dog. Kicked him right back toward the car. The dog yelped, and I felt real sorry for him, watchin' him cower back toward the station wagon."

"So what did Mott do that makes you think he's capable of murder?"

Mr. Gruber looked at me and let out a kind of a whistle, a low descending sound, and then grinned. "What are you, some kind of detective? You got a lot of questions, girl."

Rats. Anything I could think of to say would sound so incredibly stupid that I didn't say anything. I tried a shrug, and sat there, as if I had no doubt Mr. Gruber would continue on his own. Of course, I knew he wouldn't. And then, to my surprise, he did, with the whole story sort of tumbling out at once.

"Mott stood up, and I could tell he was real mad. I thought maybe he was goin' to punch Karp, and I hoped he wouldn't, because Karp coulda whupped the stuffin' out of old Mott. Then Mott said to Karp – I had to listen real close, because Mott sort of mumbles when he talks – 'You better not hurt that dog, no more. I'll kill you if you hurt that dog again.' And then he walked right around Karp like he wasn't even there, and opened the back door of the wagon so the dog could jump in. Well that really made Karp mad, that Mott was touchin' his car. He walked over to Mott and pulled his hand right off the door handle, and slammed the door. Then he got this strange look on his face, like he was talkin' to a child, or somethin' – real patronizing, like. He said, 'You like this car, don'tcha, Mott? Why, maybe I could sell you my car, and get me a truck. What do you think, Mott? You think you could drive a car?' Then he said, 'You come by my place, we'll talk about it. But you leave that dog alone. You hear, me?' Then he shook his head, said something about Mott bein' a dimwit, and he came into the restaurant."

Mr. Gruber stood up and put his empty Coke bottle into the rack by the back door. "I could tell he didn't mean it... he was goin' to play a trick on Mott, or somethin'. But I think Mott took him seriously. I know he watched him come into the restaurant, and then he stood there, lookin' at the car for a long time before he went back to his flowers. And they was all squished, and I could tell he was real upset."

I took a drink from my bottle and thought about what Mr. Gruber had said.

Maybe Mott did do it.

Stop it. Stop thinking that way. If you don't believe in him, no one will.

I drained the last of my Coke and handed the empty bottle to Mr. Gruber. "So you *really* think Mott killed Karp?" I asked.

Mr. Gruber shrugged. "Seem's pretty likely, don't it?"

I found myself nodding as I climbed back onto my bike.

11. Kay

The summer days passed, and I continued to take care of Mott's mice, visit the library, and play in the swimming hole with Blackie. I also spent a lot of time fretting about my helplessness. But I'd exhausted the suggestions in *You Be The Detective*, and I was half convinced Mott actually *had* done it.

One day, walking back to our trailer from the swimming hole, Blackie took off after Tig, Kay Gregory's cat. I chased him halfway around the residential loop before I caught him. Tig jumped onto the porch railing of Mrs. Gregory's mobile home and eyed the dog disdainfully. Mrs. Gregory stood on the porch watching. She was a friendly, white-haired woman who always wore pastel gardening clothes.

"I'm sorry," I said, shooing Blackie back in the direction of our trailer.

Mrs. Gregory smiled. "Don't worry about it, Dani. Blackie's just lucky he didn't catch Tig. I don't think he'd like the reception he'd have gotten."

"Yeah. I don't think Blackie knows much about cats. Except they're fun to chase, but maybe not to catch."

Mrs. Gregory nodded. "Would you like some lemonade? I just made a fresh batch."

Lemonade sounded good, but I really didn't like going into the Gregory's trailer. It was always so dark, and Mr. Gregory gave me the creeps. He was a World War II veteran who'd lost several fingers in battle. He also had some kind of eye disease, which was why the trailer was always kept so dark.

"Lemonade would be good, but could we sit on the porch?" I said. Mrs. Gregory cocked her head questioningly, and I quickly added, "I'm kind of sandy."

She nodded, and went in through the sliding door.

In a minute she returned and handed a glass to me where I'd settled myself into one of the lawn chairs on the porch. I pushed the heels of my flip-flops against the deck and they fell off, leaving a line of sand on the freshly-swept boards. I brushed it into the cracks with the balls of my feet.

Mrs. Gregory took a seat beside me and sipped her lemonade. She pulled her gardening gloves from the pocket of her shirt and set them on the end table, then propped her feet up next to them. "That's better," she said. "I'm too old for all this weeding."

"But your garden is beautiful," I said. "It's definitely the best one in Trailer Isle."

Mrs. Gregory smiled. "Why, thank you, dear."

"You should offer to help with the planters in town. They're looking kind of ratty, now that Mott's not around to take care of them."

"Oh, I definitely don't have the energy for that!" Mrs. Gregory said. "I can barely keep up with this little plot of land." She was quiet for a moment, and then she sighed. "Poor Mott."

"Yeah," I said. I sipped at my lemonade and watched a bee flit from one azalea blossom to the next. "Mrs. Gregory?" I said.

"Yes?" She turned toward me.

"Do you think Mott killed Karp Stegner?"

She looked at me for a moment, and I guess I wasn't expecting it when she asked me, "Do you think so?"

"No," I said automatically, but I found I couldn't look her in the eye as I said it.

"Why not?" she asked.

I swirled the ice around in my drink. "I'm not sure I can give you a good reason why I think he's innocent. But I do know everyone thinks he's guilty just because he's different. I don't think that's right."

Mrs. Gregory was quiet for a long while, and when she spoke, her voice was so soft I could barely hear it. "Let me tell you a story."

Her fingers traced the pattern of flowers on her sleeve as she spoke. "I was just a teenager when I met Harold – Mr. Gregory. We had a lot in common. We loved hiking, travel, gardening – lots of things. We had many friends, and always seemed to be doing things together with them."

She took a sip of her lemonade and continued. "But soon after we were married, the war broke out and he went off to fight. When he came back I hardly knew him. He'd lost more than just a few fingers during his time over there, although he could never really put into words what it was like. It took a long time before we could even have much of a conversation together."

I wondered what this had to do with my question, but it was kind of interesting. I'd never really thought of Mrs. Gregory as a young woman, or her husband as a young man. I couldn't really even imagine what he must have been like, when he went off to war.

Mrs. Gregory took another sip of her lemonade, and sat quietly looking at the garden. There was a spade lying half-buried in one of the flowerbeds, and I resisted an impulse to go down and pull it out. Instead I said, "But you did eventually patch things up. Here you are together, after all these years."

Mrs. Gregory nodded. "Yes," she said. "But over the years our friends seemed to drift away. I think they sensed Harold was *different*. Perhaps it was even something as small as the missing fingers. Or, more likely, the change in his personality."

I nodded. I could see where the fingers could gross a person out. They certainly had that effect on me. "You could make new friends," I suggested. Someone who didn't care about the fingers, I thought.

Mrs. Gregory sighed. "When his eyesight started to fail it was hard to make new friends, because there wasn't much we could do together." She tipped her lemonade glass up, but the liquid was all gone. A single piece of ice, half-melted, slid down against her lip, then back to the bottom as she set the glass down.

"And so we've spent our time together, and I've pretty much taken care of him these last twenty years," she said. Her voice was firm, not sad, as she finished.

I nodded. She hadn't really answered my question, but her story made Mrs. Gregory and her husband seem a lot more real to me, somehow.

She smiled at me. "I guess I haven't answered your question, have I?" She glanced at her empty glass of lemonade on the end table, then back at me. "What I'm saying is I know what it's like for a person to be *different*. Just because people are different doesn't mean they don't deserve to be treated fairly. It's a matter of justice."

I set my glass down beside hers. "'A matter of justice.' That's what my detecting book said...*Putting Together A Case: A Matter Of Justice.*"

Mrs. Gregory was watching me. I couldn't tell if she was taking me seriously or not, and now I wished I hadn't mentioned the detecting book. She probably thought I'd completely missed the point of her whole story, which I hadn't. I wanted her to see I did understand. "The police putting together Mott's case *aren't* being just," I said. "They're trying to find someone to blame."

Mrs. Gregory was thoughtful for a moment. I wondered if she was still thinking about her husband, or if she was contemplating what I'd said.

"Maybe you should talk to Mott," she said, "if you're so convinced he's innocent. Or find out what the police have done with him, anyway."

It was so obvious I could have kicked myself for not thinking of it on my own.

"You're absolutely right," I said. "I need to see Mott, and get his help to prove he's innocent." I slipped my feet back into my flip-flops and stood up. "I'll ask my Dad to take me to Visalia tomorrow."

"Your Dad may not be too wild about the idea of you associating with an accused murderer," she said. Her eyes sparkled and the sunlight made crinkly valleys of the laugh lines as she smiled. I wasn't sure if she was taking me seriously or not, but she seemed to be.

"I'll find a way," I said. "If I don't stand up for Mott, nobody will."

12. Lawyer

Wednesday came and it was time for Dad's weekly trip to Visalia. Stephanie would get dropped off at the mall. Not my idea of fun.

But this week I had a special errand planned.

When I finished feeding Flicker I dressed in my nicest slacks. After experimenting with several hairstyles I finally ended up piling my hair on top of my head in a tight, professional-looking bun. For what I had in mind I'd need to look as businesslike as possible. Now I just needed to enlist Stephanie's help. Not only did I need my sister's moral support, but I was frankly afraid of wandering around Visalia on my own. I suppose that was silly, but coming from L.A. I was conditioned to be careful. Safety in numbers, I guess.

My sister was nowhere to be found. Even as my father loaded his briefcase and an empty propane tank into the trunk, Stephanie still hadn't shown up. Was she really going to miss the trip, this week of all weeks?

"Hang on just a minute," I said. Dad eyed my outfit with interest as I hurried down to the travel trailer loop to see if my sister was at the Patterson's.

She was. Four kids were squeezed in around the dinette playing a noisy card game called *Pit* that seemed to involve everyone trying to trade cards with everyone else, all at once, and at the top of their lungs.

I grabbed my sister by the arm and tugged her out the door and down the steps, where we could talk in relative privacy.

"What?!" Stephanie said.

"Aren't you going to Visalia, today?" I asked.

"What's the point? It will just make me feel bad about the sweater I want, and I haven't got a cent."

"None?" I asked. "What happened to your money?"

"Huffaker's, that's what happened to it." Huffaker's Country Candies was the sweet shop up the main highway.

I shook my head. This was not good. I'd never have the guts to do what I'd planned without Stephanie's help. But how to get her to town?

"There's something I want you to do for me," I said.

"Yeah? What?" asked Stephanie suspiciously.

"Run an errand in Visalia."

"Get Dad to do it."

"Dad won't do it. We've got to do it on our own."

Stephanie looked at me darkly. "Does this have something to do with Mott?"

I nodded.

"Absolutely not," Stephanie said. "I don't want to have anything to do with that weird old...murderer. And anyway," she added, "you know we're not supposed to leave the mall."

"Stephanie, I've got to," I insisted, but my sister just shook her head.

I studied her, trying to think of a way to overcome her reluctance without it costing me two year's savings. But nothing else came to mind, and at last I made the offer I'd been saving for emergency use only. "I'll buy you the cashmere sweater," I blurted.

Stephanie's eyes widened. "What?"

"If you do what I want, I'll buy you the cashmere sweater you've been wanting. You know you'll never save enough for it yourself."

"Are you serious?"

"Deadly," I said, tugging on her arm. "But we've got to go *now*."

"Okay, Okay," Stephanie said, pulling her arm away. She followed me back to the trailer and waited while I rummaged for money in the back of my sock drawer.

It wasn't far to Visalia, but the ride seemed to take forever. I watched the orange trees slide past the window and tried to stay out of the hot sun. Finally my dad pulled off of the main highway and turned into the mall parking lot.

"Drop us off in front of Lerner's" Stephanie said. "That's where the cashmere sweater is."

After we climbed out, I waited for Dad's car to turn out of the parking lot, then dragged Stephanie to the bus stop.

"What about the sweater?" she said.

"We'll get it when we come back."

It took us a while to figure out which bus to take to get to the police station, but we were lucky and found one that didn't require a transfer. In less than a half-hour, we stood in front of the imposing stone building. Stephanie pulled open one of the front doors, and I stepped into the reception area.

The front desk of the police station was an immense dark wooden thing, so high I could barely see the policeman who sat there talking on the phone. When he hung up, I stood on tiptoes and spoke to him. "I'd like to see Mott Simon, please."

The man leaned forward and looked first at me, then at Stephanie. "Who?"

"Mott Simon," I repeated.

The man shook his head. "The name doesn't ring a bell. Is he a patrolman?"

"No," I said. "He was arrested. The sheriff told me he was here..."

The man nodded. "He probably meant he was in the county jail."

"Yes. That's what he said. The jail behind the police station."

"It faces Mills avenue. You need to go around the block to get in."

Stephanie and I turned to go, but the policeman called after us. "They won't let you in, though."

We stepped back to the desk. "Why not?" I asked.

"No minors allowed. Even if you're relatives, you need to be accompanied by an adult."

I sighed.

Stephanie walked to the door, then stopped when she saw I hadn't followed. She put her hands on her hips.

I scuffled over to one of the chairs against the wall and sat with my chin propped up on both fists, thinking. *Why was everything so difficult?*

The phone rang and the policeman answered it, then connected the caller to another extension.

I walked back over to the desk and said, "If *we're* relatives, does the adult have to be a relative, too?"

He studied me. "*Are* you relatives?"

I hesitated. "No. Just friends."

The policeman opened his drawer, pulled out a file folder, and flipped through it. After a moment he nodded and lifted out a sheet of paper, then picked up a pencil and copied something onto a smaller piece of paper. He held it out to me.

"What's this?" I asked.

"Mr. Simon's lawyer. A public defender. Perhaps he can arrange for you to see him."

"111 Court Street," I read. "Isn't that..."

The policeman nodded. "Right across the street. Most of the public defenders and prosecutors are in that building, because it's next to the Courthouse."

I smiled at him. "Thanks," I said. I turned to the door. "Come on Stephanie. Let's go see Mr. Novum."

Stephanie sighed dramatically, and followed me out the door.

***

Ben Novum's office was on the seventh floor. His name was stenciled in black letters on the frosted glass of the office door. I knocked and a voice said, "Come in."

I was surprised there was no secretary, just a single small office with an old wooden desk, a bookcase, a row of file cabinets, and two guest chairs. Ben Novum was an old man with pure white hair and a white mustache that looked like a caterpillar pasted onto his wrinkled face. He sat crumpled into an old wooden chair behind the desk. The stack of papers in front of him threatened to spill onto the floor. His wire-rimmed reading glasses had slipped most of the way down his angular nose, and he peered out over the rims. He looked surprised to see two young girls in his office. "Yes?" he said.

I had the strangest feeling he expected me to pull out a box of Girl Scout cookies. I walked to one of the guest chairs and plunked down, then waited for Stephanie to also seat herself, before I said, "Good morning, Mr. Novum. I'm Dani Deucer. This is my sister Stephanie. We're working on the Mott Simon case."

Beside me, Stephanie groaned. Mr. Novum raised his eyebrows.

Hmmm. Maybe that was laying it on a bit thick. I tried again. "Actually, we're friends of Mott, and we're here to prove he's innocent." I sensed Stephanie leaning away from me.

"Indeed?" Mr. Novum said.

Indeed. What was that supposed to mean? "We'd like to arrange to see Mr. Simon," I continued, "in order to get some information that will help us collect evidence."

Mr. Novum leaned back in his chair and pressed his fingertips together to form a steeple. He blinked at me, once, twice, then cleared his throat and said, "I'm afraid you girls are on a bit of a wild goose chase. Mr. Simon has decided to plead guilty."

I jumped up and heard my chair clatter to the floor. "What?!! He can't do that! He didn't do anything—"

"As his counselor, I assure you he can, and he will. After gathering the facts in the case it is our considered opinion that by pleading guilty to manslaughter by way of mental incapacity, Mr. Simon can most probably be assured of a sentence of no more than fifteen years in the county mental health facility at—"

"Fifteen years!" I cried. "Mott probably won't even live fifteen years. Does he even understand what this means? Did he say he was guilty? Or did you just talk him into it?"

Mr. Novum eyed me impassively. "That would come under the category of privileged client attorney communication. But after speaking to the prosecutor I can assure you we're prepared—"

"The prosecutor can't know what Mott is like. Has he even met him? Does he know that Mott doesn't understand what he's agreeing to?"

Mr. Novum pressed his lips together. He glanced at the door.

I stood up, pulling Stephanie with me. "Who is the prosecutor?" I asked. "We'll talk to him directly."

Mr. Novum hesitated, then said, "Miles Ketchel. Tenth floor." He sniffed. "I'm sure he'll be simply delighted to see you."

13. Prosecutor

It was nearly two o'clock when we found the prosecutor's office on the tenth floor. It took me ten minutes to convince the reluctant Stephanie to even get into the elevator. "Mortified," she kept saying. "I'm positively mortified."

A man was just stepping out of the office and locking the door behind him as we approached.

"Mr. Ketchel?" I asked.

The man turned to us and smiled. He was tall and thin, with closely cropped brown hair. He wore an expensive looking dark suit, and a gold watch. "Yes?" he said.

"I'm Dani Deucer. This is my sister Stephanie. We're friends of Mott Simon."

The prosecutor looked puzzled for a moment, then his face cleared. "Oh, yes. The trailer murder. I'm sorry," he said, his voice turning somber.

I wasn't sure what he was sorry about. That we were friends of a murderer? Or that Mott didn't have a chance? Uncertain of the best approach, I decided to try a different tack than the one that went so badly with Mott's attorney. "Mr. Novum says Mott is going to plead guilty. Is that right?"

Mr. Ketchel nodded. "That's my understanding."

"When will that happen?"

"Mmmm, in a few days, at the hearing. The clerk of the court could tell you exactly."

"Will there be a trial?"

"Probably not. Not if he pleads guilty. Just a sentencing."

"When will that be?" I pressed him.

He smiled. "That's harder to say. A month or so, I imagine."

A month! I might not even still be in Three Rivers by then. School would be starting back in L.A, and I'd be heading back, right after Labor Day. Why did everything have to take so long? And what could I do about it, anyway?

"Mr. Ketchel, do you think Mott's guilty?"

"I assume so. Innocent people don't generally plead guilty."

"Did you know that Mott's kind of...slow?"

Mr. Ketchel shook his head. "No. No, I didn't. I haven't actually met him, myself..."

I looked at Stephanie. How could he prosecute somebody he hadn't even met?

"It's actually good if he's somewhat impaired," continued Mr. Ketchel. "The court will probably go easier on him—"

"But Mott's innocent!" I exclaimed.

The prosecutor put his hand on my shoulder and spoke gently. "How can you be so sure? Do you have any evidence?"

I felt myself close to tears, but I fought them down. I'd lose all credibility if I cried now. "No," I said. "But I know him. Why can't anybody but me see that Mott's innocent?"

"I don't see how you can say that. He argued with the deceased. He was the deceased's closest neighbor. His fingerprints were all over the car – on the tailgate handle, the rear door, the steering wheel—"

"The ignition key?" I asked.

The prosecutor was suddenly quiet. His mouth was still open, as if he were still building his case, but no words came out. He stopped, and eyed me levelly.

There was something odd here. Something to do with the key? "What?" I asked.

He was silent, his eyebrows knotted in a frown. Then he shook his head and said, "I'm really not supposed to discuss the case outside of the courtroom. I'm sure all of your questions will be answered at the hearing."

He turned to go, but I called out, "Wait!" He turned back.

I studied him. What was the oddest thing possible about the key...? I gambled. "There wasn't any key, was there?" I said softly.

The prosecutor opened his mouth to speak, then closed it. Without answering, he turned on his heel and strode down the hallway.

"Did you see that?" I asked Stephanie.

"What?"

I turned to her. "He knows there's something wrong with the case. How could someone have driven the car off the cliff if there was no key in the ignition?"

"He didn't say there was no key. Besides, maybe Mott took it with him," suggested Stephanie.

"What? After crashing over a cliff he took the key out of the ignition before dragging his broken body back up to the top?" I shook my head. "And why isn't Mott injured? Or why didn't they find the key on him?"

Stephanie shrugged. "Maybe he threw it away."

"No. Somebody pushed that car over the cliff. They didn't drive it."

"You're making a lot of assumptions," Stephanie said.

"So are the police," I said.

Stephanie looked at her watch, "And Dad is probably *assuming* we've both been kidnapped, by now. Come on, let's get going." She turned and ran down the hall, with me on her heels.

***

Perhaps our father was overly complacent, or maybe he was just used to waiting for two teenage girls, but he didn't seem surprised when we showed up at the mall entrance an hour late. He *was* surprised we weren't toting any shopping bags, though.

"No cashmere sweater?" he asked Stephanie. She flopped into the back seat of the car and sat in sullen fury.

The car was silent as Dad maneuvered us onto the highway that ran, razor straight, toward Three Rivers. Then he looked over at me, and said, "Why so glum?"

I sighed, and put my feet up on the dashboard.

"Dani's been playing detective," muttered Stephanie, from the back seat. "And she doesn't like the way reality keeps interfering."

Dad was silent for a minute, digesting this. "Want to tell me about it?" he asked.

I shrugged. What was the point?

"You know," he said, "when we came up here for the summer I thought it would be a great adventure for you girls. A place safe enough for you to have free rein, sort of like I did when I was your age." He glanced over at me again. "But lately you don't seem to be having much fun. I'm worried about you. Is it that murder?

Did it scare you so you're afraid to go out and wander?"

There was a snort from the backseat. I spun around and barked, "Just shut up, Stephanie!"

"Dani," Dad said, his voice tight but restrained, "Behave. Something's obviously wrong. Now what is it?"

I crossed my arms and sat huffily staring out the window.

What difference did it make? I might as well tell him. I was probably in trouble, anyway.

"The murder is what's bothering me," I said. "Not because it scared me. Because it wasn't a murder. The police are railroading Mott. He didn't do it."

"How do you know?"

"Because he wouldn't. He couldn't. He's too nice. I know him. And the prosecutor said—"

"The *prosecutor*?"

Uh oh. Now I was in for it. I swallowed, and launched myself into the abyss. "We went to the police station today to see him. They wouldn't let us, but they gave us the name of his attorney. He's an old scumbag who's forcing Mott to plead guilty. So we went to see the prosecutor. We found out they don't even have a key for the car—"

"He didn't say that," piped up Stephanie.

I plunged on, "We think they don't, anyway. So Mott couldn't have driven it off the cliff. And the sheriff didn't say he'd been hurt, so he would have had to jump out of the car before it went over the edge, while pulling the key from the ignition, which he couldn't have done, because he's old and frail, and he *wouldn't* have done something like that anyway, because he was just trying to protect Blackie from Karp when he got into the argument at the drive-in, and it's all so unfair, and there's nothing I can do about it."

I sucked in my breath and sat apprehensively, waiting for my father's reaction. I'd probably be grounded for the rest of my life.

Dad drove along in silence, and I was beginning to think I'd imagined my own outburst when he finally spoke, softly, to the windshield. "You girls did all of this today?"

"Yes, Dad," I said. "I'm sorry. It was my idea, not Stephanie's. I dragged her along." Now, in spite of Stephanie's moodiness over not getting the sweater, I was sorry I'd taken her along. Stephanie didn't deserve to be punished.

More silence.

I glanced at Dad. He drove with both hands on the wheel, staring intently ahead. What was he thinking?

At last, he cleared his throat, and said, "You two should have told me where you were going. Why didn't you?"

I rubbed my hands nervously on the upholstery. I'd learned that honesty was best in situations like this. I turned to my father and said, "Because you wouldn't have let us."

He nodded. "You're probably right. And why wouldn't I have?"

Because he thought Mott was guilty? Wrong answer. Definitely wrong answer. "Because it was dangerous."

Dad nodded again. So far, so good.

"So," he said, his tone lightening up, "what's next?"

"Huh?" I turned to look at him, and Stephanie sat up in the back seat. Was that it? No shouting? No punishment?

"What's next?" he repeated. "If this guy's innocent, how do you prove it?"

"You mean you believe me?"

"I don't disbelieve you. I remain to be convinced."

I was stunned. He was giving me a shot to really help Mott. But how? What could I possibly do without any more evidence? And how could I collect any more evidence without talking to Mott? "The first thing we need to do is go to the hearing and see what happens. And try to talk to Mott."

"When is that?"

"Pretty soon, according to the prosecutor. I'll call when we get home and find out."

"All right," Dad said. "But this time, I'm going with you."

The one place where a man ought to get a square deal is in a courtroom, be he any color of the rainbow, but people have a way of carrying their resentments right into a jury box.

—*To Kill a Mockingbird* by Harper Lee

14. Court

I'd always imagined a courtroom would look something like a Perry Mason set: towering wood walls and lots of railings. This one looked more like a school cafeteria. There were rows of plastic chairs for the spectators, two long tables for the lawyers, then an open space of carpet, a metal desk for the judge, and a chair next to it for the witness. One wall was lined with chairs. The defendants sat in these, waiting their turn. There were only a few, and they all wore the same blue prisoner garb. A bailiff and a guard stood at either end, keeping watch.

I led my father to the end of a row near these chairs, hoping I might get a chance to speak to Mott. There was no sign of him, and I settled into my seat to wait.

One by one, the bailiff escorted each defendant before the judge. Their lawyers entered their plea and the judge asked each defendant if that was correct. Every one of them pleaded not guilty. The judge set bail and assigned a trial date, and then they were ushered out.

I caught myself thinking of each prisoner as guilty, and realized with dismay that was probably the same reaction everyone had to Mott. The adrenalin of the morning had worn off, and I was tired of the procession of thieves and muggers.

When the prisoners had all been processed, the judge called a ten-minute recess and new prisoners were escorted in. Mott was the last in line. He looked stiff and uncomfortable in his blue prisoner garb, and he seemed confused. The group filed in along the wall and sat down.

I'd have to talk fast, before the recess ended. I moved to a seat at the end of the row nearest Mott, and my Dad followed.

"Mott," I said.

He looked up. It took him a moment to focus on me, and then he smiled. "Dani!" he said. His smile faded. "What are you doing here? They didn't arrest you too, did they?"

I leaned out into the aisle. "No, Mott, I'm fine. I came to see you."

Mott smiled again. "That was nice of you."

"I'm taking care of your mice. They've grown."

"Have they? I was worried about them. I should have let them go. But the police wouldn't let me go home."

"They're fine. I feed them every morning."

Mott nodded. "Did you take back the dog?"

"He's mine, now. Reba gave him to me"

"Oh, that's nice. I bet he's happy." Mott frowned. "That Karp is a mean man."

I grew serious. "Mott, did you do it?"

"Do what?"

"Kill Karp Stegner?"

Mott gave me a wounded look. "I didn't kill anybody."

"Well, were you there?"

"I went up like he told me..."

"Why?"

"To look at his car. He said he'd sell it to me."

"What did you do?"

"He told me to try it out, so I sat in it. But I couldn't make it go."

"Why not?"

"He wouldn't let me try it. Said I was too dumb to drive. Said I'd have to pay him first."

"Did you?"

"Did I what?"

"Pay him?"

"No! He wanted $4000. Where would I get $4000?"

"Then what happened?"

"He laughed at me. I wanted to go. He made me feel real bad. But then I saw the dog. I wanted to play with the dog. The little boy was playing with him. I wanted to. But Karp shouted at us and told us to stop. I left while Karp was still shouting. Shouting hurts my head."

Mott's lawyer, Ben Novum, stepped between us. "You'll be first after the recess," he told Mott. "Come forward when your name is called."

The lawyer scowled at me, then walked to the long table at the front of the room.

Dad leaned around me and asked Mott, "Where did you go after you left Karp's?"

"I walked back to my place," said Mott.

"When was this?" asked Dad.

"The day before Dani came to visit."

"Did anything else happen?"

"Not until they came and brought me here."

The clerk called court back into session, and Mott's name was called.

"Geez, Mott. I don't know what to do," I whispered.

"Just feed my mice, will ya?"

I heard the jingle of the Bailiff's keys as he approached. My Dad pulled me back out of the aisle.

"Sure, Mott. Sure I will. You take care, okay?"

Mott nodded, and then the Bailiff was escorting him to the front of the room.

I sat back and shook my head. Now I knew how Mott's fingerprints got on the steering wheel, but that wasn't going to help. No one would believe it. What could I do? I really hadn't learned anything useful.

Things were pretty much a blur as I watched Mott's lawyer plead guilty for him. Mott nodded his head in agreement when the judge asked if he understood. He was bound over for sentencing, scheduled for the week after Labor Day.

I'd be back in L.A.

My Dad led me from the courtroom in tears.

What had I accomplished? I'd talked to Mott, and was more convinced than ever that he hadn't killed Karp. But Mott hadn't told me anything I could use to prove it. And my time was running out.

The drive home was silent, except for the whine of the wheels on the long, straight road.

15. Wreck

The sharp smell of pine clung to my fingers, mixing with the taste of the peanut butter in an odd, but not unpleasant way. Watching my family sharing lunch at the picnic table under the branches of the giant sequoia tree, I reflected on how different my home life was than that of Reba and Ardy Stegner.

My father never raised his voice. And he seemed genuinely interested in what his daughters had to say. He'd taken me to the hearing, even though he thought it was pointless.

I looked at Mom. Karp's children hadn't even *had* a mother. Stephanie said she left because of Ardy's autism – he required too much attention. I couldn't imagine Mom giving up on anything once she started.

People said I took after her. Maybe that was why I refused to give up on Mott. Something deep inside me told me he was innocent. And once I'd made up my mind about that, my path was set.

In the two days since the hearing my dreams had been filled with images of innocent people pleading guilty to crimes they didn't commit. Just last night I'd awakened Stephanie by talking in my sleep, repeating, "But he didn't do it," over and over as I tossed and turned.

"But what if he *did* do it?" Stephanie asked, when she'd awakened me. Once again she listened impatiently to my arguments about Mott's innocence.

"But he *did* plead guilty," Stephanie said. "Even Mott must know the difference between right and wrong."

"Of course he does. But he doesn't understand what will happen to him. He's just doing what his lawyer told him to do."

Stephanie sighed. "But there's nothing you can do about it, Dani. He's already entered a plea, and there's no evidence to convince people he's innocent."

"I'll find some," I said. It was a long while before I could get back to sleep.

A hot breeze rustled the pine needles overhead. It was a hundred degrees today, and bone dry, but under the trees it was bearable. I looked at the sequoia nearest us. It was a small one, barely a dozen feet around. Maybe only a few hundred years old, I guessed. We'd seen some really big ones earlier in the day.

When my father suggested this picnic I'd resisted, wanting to stay and work on Mott's case.

"But you didn't really learn anything new at the hearing," he said.

It was true. And I didn't know what to do next. So reluctantly I'd agree to come.

Now I was glad I had. The place really was beautiful. So old, and established, it gave me a feeling of contentment I hadn't experienced in a while.

I flipped the last of my bread crust to one of the ground squirrels that patrolled the perimeter of the picnic site. Blackie had secured the immediate area, holding the squirrels at bay, but this one was too fast for him, and it was up the tree before Blackie got halfway to the crust.

I helped Mom pack up the leftovers. Then Stephanie and I carried the cooler back to the car and we all headed down the twisty mountain road into Three Rivers.

In town, Dad pulled the car into Pat O'Connell's service station. We'd known Pat when he lived in Los Angeles.

An attendant came out to pump the gas.

"Is it okay if I stretch my legs?" I asked.

Dad nodded and I climbed out. Blackie and Stephanie followed. Stephanie headed into the station, where there was a Coke machine.

I wandered back toward the big oak tree that shaded the junkyard behind the station. Blackie snuffled along behind, following scent trails only he could smell. There'd been a tire swing suspended from one of the oak's branches, but it had come loose and now the tire was propped against the base of the tree. I hoisted myself up onto the tread and leaned back against the trunk, watching the traffic shimmer past on the main highway.

It was busy for a Thursday, I guess because of Labor Day weekend. Our last weekend in Three Rivers. The end of the summer.

In a way, it had been the best summer ever. I'd had the run of an entire town. Yet somehow I also felt like it had been a terrible summer. Thoughts of Mott weighed heavily on me.

The attendant slammed the hood of the car and walked back to finish topping off the tank. Easing myself off the tire, I looked around for Blackie. He'd wandered back into the junkyard and was nosing around the derelict cars.

I recognized Karp's station wagon. It wasn't hard, since it had no front doors. *Hey, this might be worth closer inspection.*

I walked over to it. I hadn't really gotten a good look at it when I'd been at the accident site. It really was a hunk of junk. One of the rear windows was cracked. The hood was crumpled all the way back to the windshield which, not surprisingly, had shattered.

In the weeks the car had sat in the junkyard it was already starting to rust where the paint was chipped off of the folded metal. The upholstery was cracked. Loose tufts of stuffing oozed through, white against the faded red vinyl. The steering wheel had been removed, I suppose as evidence, and the car didn't even have an emergency brake release. It looked like it had broken off, and a cord had been tied to the shaft where it went through the firewall. The loose end hung down nearly to the ground.

"Dani!" It was my father calling.

I collected Blackie by the collar and headed back to the car. Stephanie was already in the back seat, sipping a Coke and fanning herself with a comic book. I opened the door for Blackie and climbed in after him.

Stephanie turned to me as Dad pulled the car out of the station. "Guess what Pat said?"

"What?"

"This weekend the Red Devils always come to town. They take over the old rodeo grounds, and camp out for three days."

"Red Devils?"

Stephanie gave me a disgusted look. "You know: the motorcycle club. Black leather jackets, tattoos, that sort of stuff."

"Oh." I said. I wished Stephanie hadn't brought this up, because...

"Well, I don't want you girls anywhere near there," Mom said.

There it was. I knew that was going to happen. I gave Stephanie a disgusted look. "But Mom—" I protested.

"No 'buts'. Those people are dangerous. It's no place for young girls. There'll be no bicycle riding this weekend. Do you understand?"

I sighed and slumped in my seat.

"Well?"

"Yes, Mom."

I imagined the sound of nails being driven into Mott's coffin. Was that it? The summer was over and I'd failed?

Well, Friday wasn't the weekend, was it? I could still ride my bike for one more day. There was one last chance for me to try to clear Mott. What were my options?

Options? Heck, I had nothing.

What about suspects?

I had no real reason to suspect *anyone*, but if I had to pick someone, I suppose it would be Ardy. He'd been there when it happened, apparently. Or possibly Reba. She certainly didn't seem very broken up about it.

What about Karp's sister, Irene? I didn't know a thing about her, but what could her motive possibly be? Certainly not money. It seemed unlikely that Karp had any, knowing the way he and the children had lived. Maybe the kids? Did Irene kill him to get the kids? But Irene didn't appear all that happy to have them. So that wasn't likely.

So who *did* have a motive?

Only Reba and Ardy, that I knew of. Clearly they were motivated to get away from Karp.

Were they motivated enough to kill him?

The only way to find out was to interview people who knew them.

Stephanie had said Reba hung out at Huffaker's Country Candies a lot. I'd start there, first thing tomorrow morning.

I had one day left to solve this case. After that, I couldn't ride into town.

As we headed up North Fork Road toward Trailer Isle I had the strangest feeling that I'd just missed a major clue, but for the life of me I couldn't think what it was.

16. June

Huffaker's Country Candies was a bright red building with white trim and a wooden porch. It looked like something between a Swiss chalet and Santa Claus' house.

Even though I wasn't a candy fanatic like my sister, the smell inside Huffaker's always made my mouth water. There was cinnamon, chocolate, caramel, vanilla, strawberry, and a dozen other aromas I couldn't identify.

When I stepped into the shop Friday morning Stephanie's friend June Tobler was helping a vacationer at the cash register so I busied myself by browsing through the racks of candy canes, finally selecting a peppermint cane and taking it to the register.

"Hi, Dani," June said. "Where's Steph?"

"I think she's hanging out at the Patterson's trailer. This is our last weekend, and she's trying to do all the things she never got around to all summer."

June's smile faded. "Oh. I hadn't realized you were going away so soon. I'll miss Steph."

"Yeah, it's been a great summer." I paused. "Well, some of it has..."

"What do you mean?"

"There's something that's been bothering me most of the summer, and it looks like I'm not going to be able to do anything about it. It's really driving me crazy."

June took the candy cane from me, wrapped it in white paper and stuck a piece of tape on the outside. "What?"

"It's about Mott Simon, that guy who lived under the bridge up the North Fork."

"The murderer?"

"Yeah. That's the problem. I don't think he is."

"Why not?"

"He just doesn't seem like the type. I've been trying to find some evidence that would clear him all summer. But my time's just about run out."

"What sort of evidence?"

"I don't know. I guess that's the problem. I don't know what I'm looking for. I guess...I guess I was hoping to prove that someone else was there when Karp Stegner died."

"Like who?"

I shrugged. I looked at June, speculatively. Was she a friend of Reba's? How would she react if I mentioned the name? On the other hand, what did I have to lose? The summer was running out. If I didn't press the issue now, I wasn't going to get anywhere.

"I was wondering...where Reba was that afternoon..."

June shook her head. "Wrong track on that one, I'm afraid."

"How so?"

"Because she was here."

"How can you be so sure?"

"I can be sure because every single day this summer until the accident Reba met Eddie Branson, right here. Because Karp forbade her to see him. And this was one place that Karp never came."

Whoa! This was news. Reba was at odds with Karp over seeing some boy? Did that give her a motive? Or the boy?

"Who's Eddie Branson?"

"You've seen him around. He's from Exeter High. He always wears a denim jacket and shades? A real slimeball. But Reba liked him. And Karp didn't. I heard Karp shouting at him down by the drive-in one day, telling him to keep away from his daughter. Kind of funny, isn't it?"

"What?"

"That somebody could be too low class even for Karp?"

I nodded. I'd never heard of this Eddie guy, but he was shaping up to be a pretty good suspect. Maybe he killed Karp so he and Reba could be together. Maybe Reba put him up to it. If so, was Reba still seeing him? Or had Irene put a stop to it?

"Does Reba still meet him here?" I asked.

June shook her head. "Not since the..." She fiddled with some price stickers.

"What?"

She looked at me thoughtfully. "Can you keep a secret?"

"Probably not," I answered. "Not if it's about the murder, anyway."

She rearranged some of the jars on the counter. "It's not. It's about...Reba. Something I know she wouldn't want me to tell. But it's been bothering me."

I wasn't sure I should promise to keep a secret before I knew what it was. If it was something really bad...but I did need information. "I'll try to keep it. If I can, without hurting anyone."

June nodded. "Well, that's honest, anyway." She lowered her voice and leaned toward me. "Do you remember that fire behind the drive-in, the one that burned down the restroom?"

I nodded.

"Well, every day, Reba and Eddie used to meet here at the candy shop. Then they'd go out behind the drive-in and smoke cigarettes. Reba told me once she hated them, but Eddie told her it made her look cool. Anyway, Karp said not to do it, told her he'd whip her if he caught her at it. 'Course he told Reba he'd whip her if he caught her with Eddie, too. So anyway, they'd hide in the restroom, and smoke."

June paused and looked around the shop, although no one could have come in without us noticing. Then she continued. "After the murder, Reba moved into town, to Irene's apartment. The very next day the restroom burned down. Later, when I saw Reba, I joked about her not having a place to smoke with Eddie new. She told me she wouldn't be seeing Eddie anymore, that she was really mad at him. That he'd done something awful and wouldn't 'fess up to it."

My eyes opened wide. "He murdered Karp?"

June quickly shook her head. "No, silly. He burned down the restroom."

"What?!"

June nodded. "The day after the murder, Reba was kind of upset, even though she didn't really let on. She and Karp had never gotten along, but he *was* her father. Anyway, she told me Eddie was trying to impress her, flicking lighted matches into the trash can in the restroom. One of them caught some paper towels on fire. Reba tried to put it out but it flared up really fast. Eddie didn't even act like he cared. He was just laughing, and thought it was really funny when Reba burned her hand trying to pull the trash can out of the restroom. Then the wall caught, and she just started running."

I tried to hide my disappointment over losing my prime suspect. Was it possible the restroom fire was some kind of elaborate cover for the murder? That seemed a little too complicated, even for a Perry Mason episode. Anyway, it happened the day *after* the murder. And it seemed pretty likely that people would confirm Reba was in town on the day of the murder. The fire made sense, now that I thought about it. Reba seemed to be favoring one hand when I talked to her behind the market that day.

"Does Reba still see Eddie?" I asked.

June shook her head. "I think between Karp's death, and the fire, and living with Irene, Reba has realized she'd become kind of a loser. The last month or so, she's actually been helping Irene out with some of her work. I even saw her in the library one day." June smiled. "And I haven't seen Eddie since the fire." She handed me my wrapped up candy cane. "It's kind of funny, when you think about it."

"What?"

"It seems like Karp's death accomplished what he couldn't manage to do in life. It straightened Reba out."

Karp's death may have straightened Reba out, but it had certainly ruined Mott's life. I nodded and thanked June, then stepped out onto the front porch.

The Labor Day traffic was definitely building on the highway. I slipped my leg over the bicycle seat and pulled onto the road. As I waited for a break, a squadron of motorcycles roared past, piloted by leather-jacketed Red Devils. I covered my ears, waiting for the din to subside.

17. Reba

Reba answered the door barefoot. Behind her, Ardy sat at a card table, studying a checkerboard. He seemed oblivious to my presence.

"Hi, Reba," I said.

She looked me over. "Hi. How's Blackie doing?"

"He's fine. I'm taking him back to L.A. with me after the weekend."

Reba waited expectantly.

"Reba," I said, "Can I ask you some questions?"

"I guess. Ardy and I are kind of in the middle of a game. What is it?"

"It's about the murder. I've been trying to—"

"I don't want to talk about the murder," interrupted Reba. "It upsets Ardy."

Behind Reba, the boy stopped moving, his finger on top of one of the checkers. Still, he didn't react to my presence.

"Reba, I've only got two more days..."

Reba's eyes flashed in anger. "What business of yours is it, anyway? It wasn't your father that got killed. It was very traumatic for both of us. I'd rather not discuss it." She glared at me.

"You didn't seem that sad at the time..."

Reba put her hands on her hips. "I wasn't very together at the time. I know myself better now. And it's upsetting." She reached for the door. "Now please, leave us alone."

When the door was halfway closed I put my foot against it to stop it. Reba started to push on it but I blurted, "I know about the fire."

Reba stopped pushing and looked at me apprehensively. "What?"

"I know." I pushed the door all the way open and stepped in. Ardy slid his chair back and looked at me in alarm. "I know, but I won't say anything. I just need your help. I just need to know what happened the day Karp..."

Reba glared at me.

Consciously I softened my voice. "Look, Reba. I'm not here to cause trouble. I'm just trying to help Mott."

"Mott's guilty. He already pleaded guilty. Are you crazy?"

"I'm not crazy," I said, keeping my voice even. "I may be wrong, but I'm not crazy. Mott pleaded guilty because they told him to. That's the only reason."

Reba sighed. "That does sound like something he'd do."

"Look," I said, "will you just tell me what you know about the accident and I'll go away."

Reba took in a big lungful of air and let it out slowly, like an air mattress with a leak. "If I tell you, do you promise you won't tell anybody about the fire? I'm a different person now. If anybody finds out, everything I've done to show people I've changed will have been for nothing." Reba gave me a pleading look.

"I won't tell anyone," I said. "I think *you* should though. You didn't really start the fire, anyway, did you?"

Reba shook her head. "No. But I just don't want to deal with it. You don't know what it's like..."

She was probably right. I really couldn't imagine what it was like living with Irene. And Irene was an improvement over Karp. "Reba, I don't even know the guy who started the fire. I don't know, and I don't care. I just want to help Mott."

"You won't be able to help Mott. He was definitely there when I left. Karp told him to come and look at the car. That old hunk of junk was barely even running, but I don't think Mott knew the difference." Reba shook her head. "I can't imagine Karp really thought Mott had any money to buy a car. I think it was just one of Karp's stunts, to tease Mott. Karp loved to be mean to people. Especially people he considered inferior to himself. Which was just about everybody." Reba stuck her hands in her pockets and leaned against the door jam. "Anyway, as I told the police, Mott was sitting in the car turning the wheel like a maniac. I told Karp I was going to walk into town, and I left."

"You walked all the way into town?" I asked.

Reba shook her head. "Eddie picked me up at the Post Office. Karp didn't like Eddie, or me seeing him. So Eddie always picked me up someplace else. We went to Huffaker's, and then... the drive-in."

"Did you see or hear anything else at Karp's?"

Reba shrugged. "As I was walking down the hill, I heard Karp and Mott getting into it over the dog again. Mott was always trying to play with Blackie, and Karp hated that. He wanted Blackie to be mean, but it never worked. Ardy had been playing with him, and—"

There was a blur of motion, and Reba and I were both knocked sideways as Ardy bolted out the door.

"What the—" Reba said, stepping into the doorway. "Ardy!"

I stepped past Reba, to the railing outside the apartment. Ardy was gone.

18. Devil

I felt guilty about Ardy's disappearance. True, I hadn't even been talking to him, but clearly my arrival upset him. When Irene got home from work, she seemed unconcerned at first, saying Ardy had taken off on his own before and would be back by dinnertime. But as the evening wore on and there was no sign of him she'd finally called the sheriff.

I telephoned to check on Ardy the next day, and the next, but he still hadn't returned. Now it was Labor Day. My last day in Three Rivers. I hadn't been able to help Mott and now it seemed like I was responsible for another tragedy.

All around me Trailer Isle bustled. A park-wide shish kebab festival was a tradition for this last day of the summer season, and everyone was busy getting ready. Stephanie had been at the Patterson's since early morning, marinating the meat, cutting up vegetables, and tending several barbecues.

As the heat of the midday sun began to dissipate a volleyball game was organized in the middle of the circle and all of the kids and many of the adults came out to compete. Even my father was out there, hugging the net and spiking shots into the opposing court.

But I couldn't shake the blue funk that had settled over me since Ardy's disappearance. Mom was aware of my mood but after several attempts to cheer me failed she gave up and went to join the party. Even Blackie seemed to have deserted me. He was down badgering the volleyball players, chasing the ball whenever it escaped from the court.

For a while I sat at the picnic table in front of our trailer, listening to the distant screams of the game. Then I went for a walk around the deserted residential loop. Nearly everyone was down in the travel trailer section at the party. I saw no one but Kay Gregory, who waved at me from her kitchen window. The kids would come up later to deliver shish kebabs to her and Mr. Gregory.

I wandered out toward the Clayton's house and slipped though the gate into Flicker's pasture. The horse trotted over to me and nuzzled my hand, hoping for a sugar cube, then settled back to grazing.

I went to the tack shed and got a halter, came back and slipped it over Flicker's head, then led her back to the shed, securing her to a rail so I could curry her.

Letting my hands work on autopilot, I stewed over the events of the past months. There had to be something I was missing. Images of Mott, and Reba, and Ardy swirled before me, along with the mysterious Eddie. And yet there was so little physical evidence...a steering wheel with Mott's fingerprints, stories about Mott and Karp arguing. Was that really enough to send someone to jail for fifteen years?

Apparently it was.

There was something bothering me, but I couldn't quite put my finger on it. And that bothered me even more. All weekend long I'd moped, sullen amidst the festivities, hoping some revelation would come to me. I was sure the solution was there, but I wasn't experienced enough to see it.

When Ardy bolted, my first thought was the certainty he had murdered Karp. He had the motive, and he was there when it happened. And he was just weird enough that he might be capable of murdering his own father.

But then I thought of *To Kill a Mockingbird* again. It had been a couple of months since I'd finished it, and its story had slipped into the back of my mind. I'd mentally cast Mott in the roll of Boo, the misunderstood shut-in the world was more than ready to accuse. Bravely I'd defended Mott as an outcast in the face of opposition from all sides. Yet now I found myself accusing Ardy for the very same reasons everyone else assumed Mott was guilty. Ardy was weird, therefore he did it.

But *did* Ardy kill Karp? He was certainly acting guilty. But the police never indicated they suspected him, and deep down I knew why. Ardy's fingerprints weren't on the steering wheel.

And Ardy didn't know anything more about driving than Mott did. And Karp *was* Ardy's father, after all.

I clenched the curry brush tighter. What if Mott really *did* do it? What if I'd spent the whole summer fighting the pure, simple truth?

Then why had Ardy run? What did he see? Or do?

And *where* did he run?

I dropped the curry brush. Of course. Wouldn't he have gone home? To the only home he'd known before the murder. The sheriff would have looked there, surely. But Ardy was good at disappearing. He'd done it at the apartment the day of the fire. Maybe he hid while the sheriff was looking for him, and he was still up at the ruined trailer.

I looked at the shadows lancing across the pasture. It was miles upriver. There was no way I could walk that far and back before sunset. And my mother had been adamant about no bike riding. If I tried it and got caught I'd probably be grounded for the rest of my life. Besides, the bikes were already loaded onto the carrier on the back of the trailer, ready for tomorrow's drive home.

But there *was* a way, without breaking my word... I'd still be obeying the *letter* of my mother's law, if not its *intent*...

Before I could change my mind, I went into the tack room and pulled Flicker's saddle and bridle from the shelf.

***

The canyon looked different from the river. Wary of Mom's concern about the Red Devils, I'd kept Flicker off the road and wound my way up the riverbank, passing Mott's shack and crossing the river at a shallow spot. It took a moment for the horse to find her footing on the steep bank below where Karp's trailer had been, but soon she scrambled up. I dismounted, and tied the reins to a low tree branch. Flicker snorted in disgust at not being allowed to wander, but then settled down and began demolishing a leafy bush.

There was no sign of Ardy.

Weeds had grown up through the broken remnants of the trailer. It was nothing but a rotting pile of lumber on the rocks between the river and the terrace. High above I could see the turnout. Tire ruts were still visible where the car had plunged over the edge, but they were filled with weeds, too. Soon there'd be no sign of what had happened.

I poked around the wreckage for a few minutes with no real plan, and then started to climb up to the terrace. It was steeper than I remembered, and it took several tries before I reached the edge and pulled myself over. I stood, panting, and surveyed the place. It was covered with fill gravel and packed sand, and only a few weeds.

I tried to make out tire tracks, footprints, anything that might tell a story. At first I didn't see any, but the more I looked, the more I realized there were hundreds of them. The whole terrace was a jumble of tread marks, indentations that might have been footprints, paw prints, little bits of litter fallen from the road – how would I ever make any sense of this mess?

I was beginning to realize what a wild goose chase I'd come on when I heard the motorcycle.

At first it seemed far away. But then I realized the canyon had masked it, and it was closer than I'd thought. I crouched down so I couldn't be seen from the road, and waited apprehensively as the roar grew. Below me Flicker whinnied nervously. I hoped I'd tied her securely.

Just when I'd decided the roar could get no louder, and must begin to diminish as the motorcycle continued past, I saw it appear over the edge of the bank above me. A man wearing a black leather jacket sat astride it, appraising the driveway that led from the turnout down to the terrace. A bushy black beard and dark glasses obscured most of his face, and he wore a small helmet, like I'd seen in old war movies. Gunning the engine, he downshifted and eased the bike over the edge, gathering speed as he descended until he hit the flat ground of the terrace and the rear tire spun around, showering me with gravel.

That was when he saw me. I'd been trying to make myself as small as possible, because I knew there was no way I could make it back down the cliff before he arrived. Now I crouched near the edge, prepared to hurl myself over if he came any closer.

He killed the bike's engine and silence enveloped the canyon. It was suddenly so still I imagined I could hear the sound of the dust settling around me.

The rider pulled off his sunglasses. "Sorry," he said. "I didn't know anyone was down here. I didn't get you, did I?"

"Get me?"

"You know, hose you down with my backwash."

"Huh?"

He grinned. His boot stabbed the ground. "Gravel," he said. "I didn't hurt you, did I?"

I shook my head.

"Good." He swung his leg over the bike and put down the kickstand, then pulled off his helmet.

I inched closer to the edge. Flicker was where I'd left her, ears cocked in our direction. How long would it take to scramble back down there and climb on?

"You're not afraid of me, are you?"

I shrugged.

The rider stuck his helmet on one of the handlebars and leaned against the seat of the bike. "I haven't seen you around here before."

What did he mean 'before'?

"You don't talk much, do you? You a friend of Reba's?"

Who was this guy? He looked vaguely familiar. Softly I asked, "Are you a Red Devil?"

The man snorted. "Red Devil! Is that what they're telling you kids?"

I nodded.

"You think there's a thousand Red Devils down at the rodeo grounds, is that it?"

Again I nodded.

He grinned. "Oh, I suppose there's a couple dozen *real* Red Devils mixed in, just for a little excitement. But most of us are just weekend motorcycle fans. We do this every weekend, although this is the big event for the year. All the different groups come together for Labor Day. This is my fifth year. I'm with a group out of Stockton. Name's Tim. Tim Beacon. I'd offer to shake your hand, but you look like you might be plannin' a high dive into the canyon, so I guess I'll stay over here for a bit. And you are...?"

I stood up. As much as I'd like to disappear, I was also dying to know how this guy knew Reba. He didn't seem very dangerous, but I wasn't going to let him get any closer. "Dani," I said.

Tim nodded. "Nice name. So what brings you up here?" he asked.

"I'm on an errand. For a friend."

"Me, too," Tim said. "You seen a little kid around here anywhere?"

I shook my head. "You mean Ardy?"

"Yeah. I promised I'd keep checking up here until he turned up."

"Are you a friend of Reba's?"

"No. Irene's. I used to be married to her."

My eyes opened wide. That's where I'd seen him before – he'd been with Irene at her apartment when I'd gone to take Blackie back, the day the restroom burned down.

Tim shrugged. "I guess my wanderlust was a bit too much for her. She complained every weekend I was off hunting, or fishing, or..." he winked at me, "being a Red Devil. I can see where she would've gotten tired of it." He brushed the dust out of his beard. "Anyway, we still keep in touch. She told me about Ardy. So I've been coming up here every day to see if there was any sign of him."

So Ardy *hadn't* been here. Another dead end. I sighed.

"So," Tim continued, "what are *you* doing here?"

I said it into the ground, hoping he wouldn't ask me to repeat it, but he did. "I'm trying to solve a murder," I said again.

"I thought Irene said they'd caught the guy."

"Oh, they caught him, all right. But he didn't do it."

"How do you know?"

I looked up. "I just know him. He wouldn't have." When I saw Tim's doubtful expression I added, "And the evidence doesn't add up."

"Oh? Try me."

"They say my friend drove the car off the edge of this terrace and smashed it into the trailer," I said. "But not only does he not know how to drive, I'm pretty sure they didn't find any keys in the car. So he couldn't have driven it."

Tim walked to the edge and looked down. "What a mess." He turned and looked back up at the road. "Well, unfortunately for your friend, it wouldn't matter whether there were any keys or not."

"Why not?"

"The ground slopes down here. All he'd have to do was release the emergency brake, and the car would have rolled right off."

I opened my mouth to speak, then closed it again. Was that what happened? Had Mott released the emergency brake and then jumped out? If so, why hadn't he said so? Was that why he pleaded guilty?

"Were your friend's fingerprints on the car?" asked Tim.

I nodded.

"That doesn't look good. Where were they?"

"On the steering wheel."

"And the emergency brake release?"

No one mentioned that when we were in Visalia. I thought back to Thursday, when I'd looked at the car behind Pat's service station. There hadn't been a brake release, had there? An odd thought occurred to me, but I set it aside and asked Tim, "Do you think there's any way of telling the sequence of events from these tracks?" I pointed at the tire marks where they went over the edge.

Tim squatted above them and peered down. After a minute he shook his head. "Probably not. When I'm hunting, I look for which prints are on top of which. Like here," he said, pointing to a spot when the tire marks started down the slope. "You can tell that a dog stepped here *after* the car went over. Other spots, you can see a print half covered by the tread, which would be something that happened *before*. But over there," he said, gesturing toward the terrace, "there's been too much traffic, and the ground's too hard. You'd never figure out much from that."

Tim stood and brushed off his jeans. "Well," he said, "I'd better get back, or there won't be any food left, the way that mob goes at it."

I hadn't noticed how long the shadows were growing. I needed to get back, too. "Thanks, Mr. Beacon," I said, extending my hand.

He shook hands with me and said, "I'm sorry I couldn't be more encouraging. But I'm afraid your friend's in a difficult spot."

I nodded. "He is. And I'm afraid I can't get him out of it. But I did learn something."

"What's that?"

"That I shouldn't judge a book by its cover," I said, pointing at his jacket. "Even if it *is* leather."

Tim was grinning as he headed back to his bike. I turned and picked my way carefully down toward the river.

19. Ardy

The sun was just slipping behind the hill as I finished currying Flicker. The sounds of the Labor Day party were evident in the distance, but I couldn't stand the thought of being festive. I just wanted to be alone. It wouldn't be dark for another hour. Maybe I could go somewhere and think.

I walked past the Clayton's house and through the woods to the old barn – or whatever it was. My summer had started here. Somehow it seemed a fitting place to end it. Opening the door, I slipped inside and pulled it closed after me. It was dark inside but there were enough slivers of sunlight sneaking in through the cracks that I could easily make out the old stage, once my eyes grew accustomed to the dimness. I walked over and sat down on it, then lay back, staring at the shadows of the rafters.

It had been quite a summer. I imagined the expressions on my schoolmate's faces when I described all of my adventures. True, I'd been frustrated for much of it, but still, it had been a blast. If only...

There was a rustling noise and I got up quickly. If there was a rat in here I didn't want to meet it.

The noise was coming from the gap between the stage and the wall. The gap was bigger than I remembered. Had the stage been pushed out since I was here? I walked quietly around...

There was a body between the stage and the wall. No, not a body. A person, breathing softly, and trying to be still.

It was Ardy.

My spirits soared. At least I'd be able to make something turn out right. But I'd have to be careful not to scare him...

"Ardy?" I said, so softly is was like a breeze sighing through the rafters.

He peeked up at me, then looked back down.

"Ardy, it's Dani. I've come to take you home."

Slowly Ardy turned over and rubbed his eyes. Even in the dim light I could tell he was covered with dirt and his face was streaked from crying. He sat up and I carefully went over to him, sat down, and put my hand on his shoulder.

"It's all right," I said. "I'm going to take you home."

Ardy sniffed. "It's blowed up," he said.

"What?" I asked softly.

"It's blowed up," he repeated. "Home. It's blowed to pieces." He looked at me. "I didn't mean for it to happen. It just happened."

I sucked in my breath. Gently I rubbed his shoulder, and softly asked, "Mean for what to happen?"

He sniffed and rubbed his nose. "The car. The car blew up the house. Smashed it to little pieces. My Dad..." He was crying again.

I ran my hand through his hair. "How did it happen, Ardy? Did you see?"

He nodded, and wiped his nose again. "That man – Mott – my Dad was shouting at him. He wanted to play with Blackie and me."

Not Mott, I thought. Please don't let it be Mott.

"We were playing tug-of-war. Blackie loves it. My Dad made Mott go. He wouldn't let him play. He was mad at me, too. He didn't ever want Blackie to have any fun. He came over and took my rope away. Then he – he hit me. I ran. I ran into the trees, to my secret place where he never hit me. Blackie followed, but Dad called him back. He kicked Blackie, and told him he was a bad dog." Ardy shook his head. "But Blackie's a good dog. He's not a bad dog. Dad went down the hill into the trailer. I wanted Blackie to come back to me, in my secret place. I watched him. But he was looking for the rope. Dad took our rope." He was sobbing now, and I could barely make out the words. "That's when the trailer blew up. There was this really loud noise, and then the car wasn't there, the trailer wasn't there..."

Ardy leaned over and put his head against my shoulder, sobbing, "And Dad wasn't there."

I held him to me, rocking back and forth, murmuring soothing words. What did it all mean? Was he telling the truth? The car couldn't just—

And then it hit me. All of the weeks of evidence collecting, interviews, and theorizing suddenly clicked into place, and I knew what happened. At Pat's gas station the car had been missing the emergency brake release handle. There was a rope tied to the shaft. And Blackie had been looking for his tug-of-war rope.

As I sat there in the old barn, comforting the crying child, I found myself smiling, almost overcome with the euphoria of having solved the crime. For I suddenly knew, with certainty, Karp had been killed by his own most abused victim. Blackie was the murderer.

And I could prove it.

Gently I turned Ardy to face me.

"Ardy," I said softly. He looked up at me for a moment, then back down at his lap.

I reached out and brushed the tears from first one cheek, then the other. "Ardy, did Blackie pull the emergency brake release?"

Ardy looked up again and sniffled. "The what?"

"Was there a rope? A rope dangling out of the car? Did Blackie pull on that rope?"

Ardy shook his head, shook it over and over. But I knew it had to be true. "Shhh," I whispered, trying to calm the frightened boy. I took his hand. Looking into his eyes I smiled encouragingly. "Ardy, are you worried Blackie will get in trouble?"

Ardy nodded vigorously. "He's not a bad dog," he insisted. "He didn't mean to do it."

"Ardy, he's just a dog. He can't get in trouble for what happened. He was just doing what dogs do. No one will hurt Blackie if you tell the truth." I squeezed his hand. "Do you understand?"

Ardy stared at me, wide eyed. "They won't take him away and lock him up? Dad always said if Blackie was bad they'd come and take him away and lock him up."

I shook my head. "No one will lock Blackie up. I'm taking care of Blackie now. I won't let anything happen to him. Do you understand?"

Ardy sniffed. He rubbed his hands together, then dried his nose on his sleeve. I waited, not wanting to push too hard. I hoped he was collecting his thoughts, that I still had his attention. Finally, when I was about to try again, Ardy let out a long sigh and began to speak.

"I understand. People think I'm stupid. But I'm not. I'm not stupid." He squeezed his eyes tightly shut. "It's just hard. Hard to talk to people. Hard to understand what they think. Or why they do the things they do." He swallowed and began to bounce the palms of his hands up and down on his knees. "I don't know why Dad didn't like Blackie. He's a good dog. Blackie didn't mean it. He just wanted his rope back. We like to play with it. Dad took it. I don't know why. He did things like that. I don't know why." He shook his head, staring off into the darkness of the barn. He sighed again. "There was another rope. A rope tied to the car. Blackie wanted it. He pulled on it. I shouted at him. I told him not to. I knew Dad would be mad if we took his rope. But Blackie wanted it. He pulled on it. Somehow – I don't know how – it made the car move. I ran. I ran to try to stop the car. I knew Dad would be mad if the car moved. But I couldn't stop it. It just went by itself. I don't know why."

Ardy stopped moving. The air from his lungs leaked slowly out in a long sigh, until he looked like someone had crumpled him in two. He stared at the floor, shaking his head.

I reached out to put my hand on his back. "It's not your fault," I whispered. "It's no one's fault. It was just an accident, Ardy."

"I knew Dad would be mad," he said to the floor. "I knew it. But then there was this loud boom, and Blackie ran, and I ran, and I couldn't find Blackie anywhere, and then—"

He was sobbing again, softly now, and I patted his back. "Go on," I said gently. "Tell me, Ardy. You'll feel better if you tell someone."

Ardy slowly sat up. "I went back to tell Dad I did it, not Blackie. I didn't want him to hurt Blackie. But I couldn't find Dad. I couldn't find him." He stared at the black wall of the barn now, seeing what I could only imagine, when he said, "And then I found him."

Ardy turned to me slowly and I saw into his eyes in a way I'd never connected with him before. "I found him," he said, "and he wasn't mad. He wasn't mad at all."

And then he slumped into my lap, sobbing as I held him and rocked him, soothing his fears and comforting him for a long, long while.

So it took an eight-year-old child to bring 'em to their senses....
That proves something - that a gang of wild animals can be
stopped, simply because they're still human. Hmp, maybe we need
a police force of children.

—*To Kill a Mockingbird* by Harper Lee

20. Detective

It was dark by the time I led Ardy out of the barn and gently coaxed him across the field to Trailer Isle. The Labor Day party had broken up and the park was quiet. Amber lights glowed in many of the windows but there was no one in sight. I could hear a sprinkler hissing softly on the volleyball court, but it was too dark to see. I wondered if I was in trouble for skipping the party, or if I'd even been missed.

I stopped in front of our trailer. Maybe Ardy would feel more at ease if he could talk out here. I knocked at the door. When I heard movement I opened it a crack and called, "Dad?"

After a moment my father opened the door and looked out, pausing when he saw the boy standing behind me.

"Dad," I said, "we've got something to tell you."

***

The next day was hot and still. All the summer visitors were gone and I was supposed to be halfway to Los Angeles. But instead, I was holding Blackie by the collar under the old oak tree behind Pat's filling station.

The men had been in Irene's apartment, taking Ardy's statement. I stood nervously watching them cross the highway, wondering how it had gone. When my Dad winked, relief tingled through me.

The sheriff and prosecutor Ketchel, and even sour old Ben Novum lined up next to Karp's car. My Dad had his camera.

Mr. Ketchel nodded and I let go of Blackie's collar. "Get the rope boy," I said, "get the rope."

I raised my arm to point, but it wasn't even halfway up before Blackie seized the end of the cord that dangled from the emergency brake and gave it a good, stiff yank. The brake went "thwack" and the car lurched forward a foot, bumping into the embankment.

"Click," went the camera.

Ben Novum stared.

"Well, I'll be damned," said the sheriff. He turned, wide-eyed, toward prosecutor Ketchel, whose mouth slowly shaped itself into a great, big grin.

* * *

Our return to Los Angeles was postponed and the start of school forgotten in the excitement of the busy week that followed. The thing I remember best was the day Dad and I drove Mott home from Visalia.

Instead of dropping him off at the bridge, Dad stopped in front of the Clayton's house. In the tack shed Mott found his gardening tools, egg cartons, a new mattress... and his mice. He got all choked up and couldn't find any words, but it didn't matter. The sparkle in his eyes said everything. We left him to settle into his new home.

***

The sun was just clearing the trees as Dad locked the door of the trailer and turned to me. "Okay, Detective Deucer," he said with a wink, "All aboard." He gestured toward the car.

"Aren't you forgetting something?" I asked.

"What?"

"Hitching the trailer to the car?"

"Don't need to," Dad said. "When I talked with Mr. Clayton about a job for Mott, he mentioned we could keep the trailer here in the residential loop during the winter for the same price as the storage yard. I already wrote him a check. That way we can use it on the weekends, whenever we like."

"That's great Dad! We can come up and see how Mott's making out."

He tossed his briefcase into the trunk and slammed it. "Did you bring Blackie a dish so we can give him some water in Bakersfield?"

I nodded. When I opened the rear door Blackie jumped in, joining Stephanie in the back seat. I climbed in and my father started the engine.

I felt a twinge of regret as we pulled away from the place I'd called home all summer. Impulsively I leaned forward and touched both parents' shoulders and said, "Thanks for a great summer, guys."

Mom turned and smiled. "You certainly have some stories to tell when you get back to school, don't you? It's not every girl who gets to spend her summer solving a murder."

"Yeah, but it was Dad who finally convinced the sheriff and the prosecutor to take another look at the case. I could never have done that on my own."

"Oh, I wouldn't be so sure of that," Dad said. "When you look at all you accomplished this summer, I wouldn't put it past you."

"Yeah," said Stephanie. "And she got us out of a week of school too." She winked at me.

Dad cleared his throat. "I think it was getting Blackie to pull on the emergency brake cord that really did the trick."

"It also helped that someone was finally willing to listen to Ardy," I said.

"But it was you who convinced Ardy to talk," Mom said. "You know, I think I've seen improvement in that boy, just in the past week. You've done him a world of good, Dani. I'm very proud of you."

"Well, hopefully that new school in Visalia will help him," I said. "He really seems to like it."

The car sent up a cloud of late summer dust and dried oak leaves as we crossed the culvert and headed down the lane next to the paddock.

As we passed the driveway in front of the Clayton's house Mott was working in the flowerbed out front. I thought about asking my Dad to stop so I could say goodbye, but it all seemed so awkward.

Mom must have read my thoughts, because she said, "You sure changed his life, honey."

A feeling of pride swelled inside me and I felt hot tears on my cheeks. I *had* changed his life, I realized.

Everyone in the car was silent until we pulled out onto North Fork Road. Then Mom turned to Stephanie and said, "Did you enjoy your summer, Stephanie?"

"It had its moments. I wouldn't mind seeing the Pattersons again. Mike said they'd be up some weekends this winter, too."

"Mike?" Dad said. Stephanie didn't answer, but I could see Mom trying to hide a smile.

"So," he said, "Do you girls still think it's boring around here?"

"I could use a little boring," I said, "after all this excitement."

"Well, we've got a four hour drive ahead of us back to L. A. That should take care of it." We both groaned. He continued, "Do you want to stop at the market and pick up a Nancy Drew mystery to read on the drive back?"

"Umm...thanks Dad. But I think I'll get something a little more serious, if you don't mind."

When we got to the store I looked through the paperback rack while Stephanie picked out a magazine. At the checkout register she leaned over to see what I had selected. *"To Kill a Mockingbird?"* Stephanie said. "You already read that."

I shrugged. Somehow I thought I might understand more of it now.

She took the paperback from me and looked at the cover. There was a photograph of a man wearing glasses. He was sitting by the bed of a little girl – Scout, I presumed.

Stephanie wrinkled her nose. "It looks boring."

I could tell she was thinking about saying something else – insulting, no doubt – but she didn't. She just looked at me for a moment, then handed the book back.

"I'll pay for it," she said.

I must have looked shocked, because she smiled sheepishly as she handed the cashier the money.

"Thanks," I said.

"Sure." She pushed open the glass door and we stepped out into the shimmering heat. "Just remember, you owe me one cashmere sweater."

"At least."

We climbed into the car and my father backed out onto the highway.

Someone had replaced the flowers in the planter in front of the market. Yellow, red and violet, the bright blossoms waved like tiny flags, celebrating their differences.

Settling back in my seat for the long drive home, I sighed contentedly. As I flipped open my book I wondered who else might need the help of Detective Deucer.

22060263R00087

Made in the USA
Lexington, KY
10 April 2013